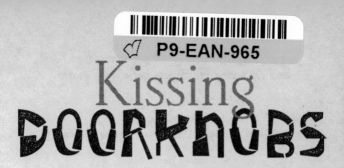

Kissing
DOORKNOBS

TERRY SPENCER HESSER

To my husband, Dennis,
for encouraging me to write the stories that I tell
and for loving me despite not a few "quirks"

Published by
Bantam Doubleday Dell Books for Young Readers
a division of
Random House, Inc.
1540 Broadway
New York, New York 10036

Visit us on the Web! www.randomhouse.com

Educators and librarians, for a variety of teaching tools, visit us at www.randomhouse.com/teachers

ISBN: 0-440-41314-1

RL: 6.1

Reprinted by arrangement with Delacorte Press

Printed in the United States of America

December 1999

10

OPM

ACKNOWLEDGMENTS

I would like to thank Susan Richman and the Obsessive Compulsive Foundation of Metropolitan Chicago for their information and encouragement; my sister, Leslie, for her humor, love, and underreaction to my adolescent compulsions; Lawrence David for being any writer's dream editor; and my daughter, Kira, for being Kira.

Although this book is not an autobiography, I have experienced some of the obsessions and compulsions that I have written about and am grateful to see and share the humor in this kind of pain.

1
Cracks . . .
Everywhere You Look

Step on a crack, break your mother's back! The first time I heard that stupid rhyme was when I was eleven years old and still in possession of my own thoughts.

At first I thought the rhyme was stupid. *Step on a crack, break your mother's back!* When I couldn't get it out of my head, I thought it was annoying. *Step on a crack, break your mother's back!* Finally I thought it was scary. But no matter what I thought about it, I couldn't stop thinking it. Actually, it was more as if I couldn't stop hearing it in my head over and over again.

I heard it while I was brushing my teeth,
Step on a crack, break your mother's back!
eating dinner,
Step on a crack, break your mother's back!
doing my homework,
Step on a crack, break your mother's back!
having a conversation,
Step on a crack, break your mother's back!
and falling asleep.

It was like listening to the sound track of a movie that I wasn't watching. A weird time-release audio torment stuck on Replay in my brain. Even now, I'm fourteen years old and just thinking about it makes me tap it with my feet. *Step on a crack, break your mother's back! Nine* syllables. *Un*even. I hate that.

Until that crack stuff hit the Replay button in my brain, I thought my life was pretty much within the bounds of ordinary. At least, by my definition of ordinary. I was tall and blond, with the high cheekbones and flat face of a Slav. I also had dark smile-shaped circles under my green eyes. I had good grades, a younger sister named Greta, two parents, my own room, a lot of friends, and even more allergies and anxieties to keep me company. Actually, my mom always accused me of being a bit of a worrywart, but we all thought I was normal. Worried, but normal. Smart. Good. Funny. And busy.

Between my schoolwork, shopping, sleepovers, talking with friends on the telephone and watching television, I had a lot to think about and a lot to do. So the last thing in the world I wanted was to think the same thought over and over and over again, especially a thought as uninteresting and a rhyme as stupid as *Step on a crack, break your mother's back.*

Not that it mattered what I wanted to do or think about. Because not long after I heard that moronic rhyme for the first time, I suddenly couldn't take my eyes off the sidewalk long enough to cross streets safely. Unexplainably, and in a state of confused foreboding, I was examining every square of pavement between my house and my school. And I was *counting the cracks.* Lots of them. At approximately 60 paved squares a block, there were roughly 480 opportunities to break my poor, sweet, understanding, gentle, funny mother's back. Actually, there were exactly 495 opportunities to break her back. And the idea of life without her, or of her lying in traction for the rest of her life, scared me so much that my upper lip would sweat whenever I thought of it—which I did with alarming frequency.

I knew that all this was totally stupid. And I knew that anyone who saw me quietly counting cracks would know that something was seriously wrong with me. So I was confused. And embarrassed. But I couldn't not think the thoughts. And I couldn't not count the cracks. And, of course, I couldn't tell anyone. Needless to say, I had to walk alone.

To and from school; I held my head down and fixed my eyes a few feet below and ahead of me. Counting. Sweating. And, of course, worrying. About my mother's spine. About my sanity. About being seen. And about being interrupted.

". . . thirty-two, thirty-three, thirty-four, thirty-five—"

"Tara!" Uh-oh.

"Thirty-six—"

"Tara, wait up!"

My heart was beating faster and faster. I hated when this happened. "Thirty-seven." Aside from the obvious embarrassment, I totally resented anyone's invading my space while I was counting.

"What are you doing?" The voice was right behind me.

"Forty-"—my mouth was so dry I could barely speak—"two."

"Tarrraaa!"

I imploded. Hostility ricocheted through my organs and oozed out of my sweat glands. I became a carbonated fury shake. I closed my eyes and clenched my fists to keep from crying.

"What's wrong?" The voice at my side was a gentle one. It wasn't mocking or mean. Slowly I opened my eyes, and tears poured down my cheeks. Emily was a girl in my class. She was in my math group. She had two brothers and a dog. She was staring at me as if I had just walked off a UFO.

"Leave me *alone*!" I yelled at her.

"Why?" she asked. "What're you—"

"Because!" I paused, wondering what to say. I was furious. And embarrassed.

"*Because* isn't an answer."

My thoughts were swimming, but I still wasn't answering her. I was just staring at the sidewalk. I'd never be able to explain this. To her or to myself. And to get the counting right, I was going to have to go home and start all over and be late for school *because of this interruption*.

"Why didn't you wait—"

"Because you're *rude*!" I screamed. "Don't you know that when you call a person and they don't answer, you're supposed to leave them alone? Don't you know that?" My voice sounded far away. Mean. Serious. I didn't recognize either the tone or the rhythm.

"But Tara—"

"And *don't* . . . don't ask me any more questions. Please! Please."

Gasping for air, I turned away from Emily. I felt as if I was in a dream or under water.

Although I'd always liked the suburb of Chicago I grew up in, it was no place to have a private problem in public. Too many people knew each other. There

4

wasn't enough space to hide embarrassing things. Suddenly there wasn't enough space for anything. Not even to breathe.

Even the houses looked as if they were hiding things. Square brick facades with closed doors to hide secrets and curtained windows threatening to reveal them. I knew that we had crazy people in our town. In fact, everybody knew exactly who most of the crazy people were. But the crazy people in our town were crazy inside their homes, behind those closed doors and drawn curtains. Not outside—like me—in front of God and everyone.

"Tara?" Emily said again.

"Shhh!" I hissed, overwhelmed by the vibrations of fear that my heart was sending into my ears.

I ran away from Emily without any further explanation and kept running all the way home. On my front porch I caught my breath, wiped the tears from my eyes and started over, counting the cracks without interruption to get it right. "Onetwothreefour . . ."

After that, to avoid public scenes and reduce the need to start over, I began to ignore people calling me as well as car horns and angry drivers shouting at me when I walked in front of their cars without noticing.

"Hey, *little girl*! If you're *blind*, get a *dog*!"

When I passed someone I knew—"Tara! Tara Sullivan?"—I'd pretend I was looking for something I'd lost and wave them away. What else could I have done? Tell them that I had a tape stuck on Replay in my brain and I was counting cement cracks?

Once, Mrs. Scott, a neighbor, actually grabbed my shoulders and made me stop counting to talk to her.

"Tara, I've been calling you and calling you. Don't

tell me you didn't hear me," she said with more than a hint of exasperation in her voice.

I smiled, although I could feel tears threatening to spill over. I hoped that if Mrs. Scott noticed, she would think they were from the cold air, and I shivered on purpose. "I'm sorry," I said, trying not to look as upset as I felt. But my emotions were already bubbling deep inside. I was going to have to go all the way home to start over. I was going to be late for school *again*. And I was afraid that my anger might explode out of my ears, nose and mouth.

"What a little space cadet!" Mrs. Scott laughed and hugged me to her chest. That was when I saw two boys from my class, Kevin and Richard. They were watching us and laughing at me.

That broke me. One tear fell down my right cheek. Unbelievably and instantly, my left cheek felt cheated! I wondered if I could make one tear fall down my left cheek the next time I got upset to keep things balanced. I worried about the time delay between the two tears. Vexed and embarrassed at the idiocy of my thoughts, frustrated that I was going to be tear-unbalanced from now on, and angry that I was going to be late for school, I started to run away from Mrs. Scott and the dozen or so kids who had joined Kevin and Richard to watch me. I felt like roadkill that was still alive. A human car wreck. I wished with all my might that it was a bad dream and I'd wake up. No such luck. I was going to have to face Kevin and Richard again when I finally got to school. I was going to have to face Emily again, who I was sure would recognize a pattern when she heard about this incident from big-mouthed Kevin or Richard. Suddenly I hated all of them. Especially Mrs. Scott.

"I gotta go. I'm late," I hollered over my shoulder.

Mrs. Scott was not an easy woman to shake. "Ta-rrr-aaa!"

I was so frustrated that tears started pouring out of both eyes. *"What?"* I yelled.

"School is that way!"

She was smiling with her mouth but her eyes were hard. She probably thought I was insane. I knew she was going to call my mother and tell her what happened. I shuddered to think what she would say about me. *I* didn't know what to say about me. I had no words to untangle the senseless mess of my thoughts and actions. I felt nauseated with shame. Kevin was laughing and pointing at me. Richard looked confused. I began to hate both of them, just for witnessing my humiliation.

"I forgot something at home!" I screamed over my shoulder, and ran. Mrs. Scott hollered something but I didn't turn around or stop until I was on my front steps. Breathless, crying, and doubled over from a cramp in my side, I took a few minutes to pull myself back together.

"I'm okay, I'm okay, I'm okay . . . I'm cracked and worried and tired. I'm scared and I have eczema. I have no idea what's happening to me but I'm okay." Sometimes the sound of my own voice calmed me down. Then, panting, sad and frustrated, I began the task that lay before me and started off for school again, counting every crack along the way and wondering for the billionth time what was wrong with me.

2
Childhood

t's a warm, sunny summer day. My friends and I are happily playing outside my house. We're chasing each other and laughing. We all feel safe and happy. Then, out of nowhere, a giant monster pops up from behind a white house a block away. It is huge and fearsome and blocks out most of the blue sky. It is so big that in one step it will not only be at my house, it will be on my house, possibly crushing us to death. My friends all scream and run. I can't run. I can't move!

I woke up screaming. I always woke up screaming from that nightmare, which I'd had over and over again, at least once a month, for as far back as I could remember. Usually, by the time I opened my eyes, my mother was already by my side, gently stroking my hair with her dry white hands and chipped nail polish. "I hate dream monsters too," she said sweetly. "But that's all they are. Dream monsters."

Letting kindness get that near to pain is like giving a fire some oxygen. Each time it happened, I cried harder and harder and harder as my eczema secretly spread to my torso and made an appearance behind my knees. Eczema is a red, scaly rash that can crop up anywhere, anytime, and itch so badly that you want to scratch it off with a chain saw. My eczema, like my worries, seemed to come and go regardless of nightmares or the terrible kindnesses.

To keep from tearing my skin off, I wore kneesocks on my arms day and night and refused to go to pre-school. If I had put shoes on my hands and walked on all fours, I would have looked like a human spider with legs missing. Kids would have laughed. My mother let me stay home with her and my baby sister.

"Shhh. It was only a dream," my mother would say calmly while pulling the kneesocks past my elbows.

"I know," I'd say, scratching my upper arms with a vengeance and sniffling like crazy. Then I'd say, "Tell me again."

"It was only a bad dream."

I'd look at my mother in a way that begged for more. "Three more times. Please!"

She complied. "It was only a bad dream. It was only a bad dream. It was only a bad dream." It didn't count. I still felt anxious. She sounded too impatient.

"*Nicely,*" I begged.

Tired and beaten, she complied.

"It's only a bad dream. It's only a bad dream. It's only a bad dream."

I searched her face for reluctance or impatience. Anything other than total sincerity ruined it and I'd have to make her do it again. She seemed sincere. She smiled and kissed my forehead. I closed my eyes and waited for relief. It came. I exhaled and pointed to the closet door. Without a word, my mother got up and shut the door. She knew I had seen green monster eyes in there before. Eventually I'd fall asleep listening to the squeak of el trains returning to the end of the line and thinking about people going home late at night. But I'd sleep so lightly I'd wake up startled from the little explosions whenever the furnace turned on. Each time I awoke, I wanted to go and sleep with my mother, but my parents didn't like it when I woke them up in the night for no reason. Instead, I'd get up and put cold washcloths on top of my bloody arms, go and look at my baby sister sleeping. And then I'd scratch my arms until morning.

Until I hit kindergarten, my mother and I spent a lot of time together. My great-grandma's cottage in Michigan was our favorite place to go before and after my sister was born. It was fun in all seasons, but summer was best.

My mom and I made sand castles in a wooden box and fed the neighbor's peacocks and peahens. While my sister slept, we played croquet on freshly cut grass and drank Dr Pepper out of bottles. We were always together. And we were happy. Looking at clouds. Rocking on the swings. Lying in the sun. We loved being busy doing nothing.

After all that togetherness, it was hard to start school. I cried every day I had to be separated from my mother. Each time she dropped me off I doubted I'd ever see her again. I doubted she would be safe until she picked me up. And I doubted the rest of our family could survive without her. Tears streaming down my face and fists clenched, I'd run to the classroom door and stamp my feet. I wanted to make sand castles with her. I wanted to drink Dr Pepper in the sunshine. I wanted to hold her hand. I didn't want to be abandoned.

Three girls in my class repeatedly hugged me when I

cried. Kristin, Keesha and Anna would eventually become my best friends, but it took me a long time to care about anyone but my mother. My eczema responded to my longing and showed up red and scaly in every crease of my skin. I scratched. I cried. I had nightmares. Then I scratched and cried some more. Kindergarten was hell.

After a few months, I got over my separation anxiety. But other things started to bother me. For instance, throughout first, second, third and fourth grades I lived in dread of fire drills and emergency evacuation practices, which my school took very seriously.

Without warning, we were periodically blasted out of our rooms by a horrible noise and taught to either huddle in the halls with our arms over our heads as protection or to march single file out of the possibly burning building.

Although the other kids performed the drills in a joyous, snickering, happy-to-be-interrupted-in-school way, I was inconsolable.

Kristin, Keesha or Anna held my hand in an attempt to calm my fears.

"Don' be ascared, Tara," said Kristin sweetly. "This can save our lifes."

"It's not real!" said Anna.

Keesha shook her head apprehensively.

We were being trained for various disasters the adults believed might befall us, like a war, a fire, a hurricane or a hostage crisis. My worst fears and gloomiest thoughts were being substantiated. The worst could happen while I was at school, separated from my family. I'd be alone. Dying, suffering, suffocating . . . by myself.

"Tara Sullivan! Don't cry, honey," said myriad kind-faced teachers who, I believed, thought of teaching as a mission, a calling or at least a room to go to where they could be the boss. "Come on, there's nothing to be afraid of."

I didn't look up. I didn't stop crying. Like a terrified animal, I froze in place.

"Tara! Look. No one else is crying. It's just practice. It's not real."

Practice. I wondered when we would use this ability to crouch on the floor with our hands over our heads. Tomorrow? In fifth grade? In high school? What were they thinking? I kept crying and worrying, worrying and crying.

There were a lot of parent-teacher and parent-counselor meetings about my fears, but no one seemed to feel confident about what to do. Everyone hoped I'd grow out of my "constant fretting," or "worrywarting," as my mother called it. As I grew older, though, my fears got worse. And so, unable to rely on any of the adults in my life to save me from my terrors about this world, I turned my attention to God and the next world.

Although my mother was not religious, my father was Irish and very Catholic. They had split the difference by sending me to public school enhanced by weekly catechism lessons starting in first grade. I'm sure neither of them could have guessed how seriously I would take my Catholicism.

From the first class, I worried about original sin, which comes from being born a human after Adam and Eve screwed up in the Garden of Eden. According to my catechism, only baptism could erase original sin. But I reasoned that if that was true, zillions of good but unbaptized people might not get into heaven. How could that be fair?

I also worried about unbaptized babies who had died. Then I worried about abortions. I wanted to collect all the aborted fetuses in the world and have them baptized to make sure the little souls got into heaven even though their fully formed bodies never made it to earth. By fourth grade, I didn't care about prochoice or prolife, but I was extremely proafterlife.

I worried about death and heaven and Judgment Day. I worried about shame, wretchedness, paralysis, disease and accidents.

I didn't like passing by the giant crucifix looming above the altar of our big old dimly lit church. It made me scared and sad. Furthermore, since we'd been taught that Christ died for our sins, I was afraid I had had some hand in his pain. Even if Christ was crucified thousands of years before I was born, I still felt queasy about my role in his terrible suffering.

It was just as hard to look at the statues of the Blessed Virgin and Joseph: I could never meet their gazes. You just can't crucify a child and then hang out with the parents—even if they are statues.

I hated the confessionals. Three dark little coffin-sized closets nailed together and hooded with dusty velvet curtains standing along each side of the pews. Not very inviting. Not very . . . forgiving.

Inside the two side cubicles, there was enough room for one person to kneel. In the middle there was enough room for a priest to sit without a lot of discomfort—assuming that he wasn't claustrophobic. There were tiny screened doors cut into the partitions between the priest and each penitent.

Once I was inside the confessional, dread danced a jig in my nervous system. My entire soul cringed with fear. The darkness and stale air were stifling. I kept my terror in check by listening to the muffled murmurs of somebody else's sins.

When the priest finally slid open the shoebox-sized door and let me know he was ready for me, I moved my lips closer to the screen.

"B-Bless me, F-Father, for I have sinned . . . ," I stammered. My heart was pounding and I felt dizzy. I was terrified.

For most Catholics, confession is a way of getting their problems off their chests, a way of apologizing to God through a priest and being forgiven. In my mind, the loop never closed that neatly.

"It's been a week since my last confession and in that time I . . . um . . . I had a nightmare. . . . ," I croaked.

"As far as I know, child, bad dreams are not a sin," the priest responded in a near whisper, probably thinking about his own bad dreams.

"But *after* the bad dream, the nightmare, I got out of bed, crept into my parents' room and silently lay down on the rug next to their bed. I didn't crawl into their bed because they don't like me coming in their bed all the time . . . even if I need to. So anyway, I must have rolled under their bed after I fell asleep, because the next thing I knew my parents were running around the house calling my name. My mother was almost crying and my dad sounded scared too."

"I see," he said, trying too hard to sound sympathetic.

"The thing is, when I heard how worried they were, I didn't come out. I stayed under the bed for a while longer. I *liked* that they were scared. I felt they needed to be punished for not letting me sleep with them when . . . when I get scared."

"So you just stayed under the bed listening to their terror?"

"Until I heard them calling the police. Then I came out."

"Hmmm."

"They were both really, really mad at me."

"Understandably. Is that all, child?"

"Um. No. Not at all," I said. I wanted to confess everything. *Everything.* I wanted to make absolutely *certain* that when I walked out of that box and finished my penance, my soul would be radiant and I'd be ready to die and go to heaven. Or at least not be doomed to hell.

"There's a lot more," I said. I felt the walls shake as the priest made himself comfortable while muttering something inaudible.

"What's that, Father?"

"Nothing. Go on, child. I'm still relatively young."

My confessions always took a lot of time. As a result, the lines outside my box often turned into an angry mob of impatient penitents. Once, the confessor on the other side of the priest passed out from kneeling and waiting so long in the heat. When I heard what had happened, I tried to get back into the box to confess my guilt in the situation, but it was almost impossible. Everyone, grown-ups included, started cutting in line in front of me. And they weren't even polite about it.

"Sorry, honey, I don't have all day," they'd mutter without looking at me. Even my friends started to cut in.

"Sorry, I've got to be home before I'm an adult," said Keesha with a smirk as she stepped in front of me.

Although the priests tried to be patient, they realized that I was more compulsive than penitent in my desire to tell everything. Every sin, every sinful thought. Occasionally they'd even try to end my confession by saying something like "You can sum this up, you know." But I'd never let them do that to my soul.

"Oh, no, Father!" I'd moan. "I want to tell you *everything*." I'm sure hearing me say *everything* sent a shiver down the spine of every priest who ever heard my confession. *Everything* meant they'd be in that box for a long, long time. First with me, then with a lot of others. *Everything* had lifelong Catholic priests wishing they were Buddhists.

3

Fifth Grade

Fifth grade started out as the best year of my life. For no reason that I could identify, my nightmares stopped, my worries lessened, my eczema was better and I was even used to the stupid drills at my school. So with all that bad stuff gone, I was suddenly feeling a lot of good things. Like love. I *loved* my family, God, my teacher Mrs. Prack; and my three best friends, Keesha, Kristin and Anna, like never before. It was as if this really good feeling had replaced all my bad ones. I felt great. Open. Present. Alive. I hadn't felt that good since feeding the peacocks in Michigan with my mother so many years before.

I learned a lot about my friends at that time. We slept at each other's houses and talked on the phone every night. It was comforting to discover that they had problems they were dealing with too. I guess I'd been assuming I was the only one in the world with problems.

Kristin was blond and lived next door to me. She was weird because she always worried about her weight even though she wasn't even close to being overweight.

17

She analyzed the fat grams of everything she put into her mouth.

Keesha was black and full of theatrical attitude. Her parents and grandparents had been part of the civil rights movement and, as she told us frequently:

"*Hawney!* My *mama* and *daddy* and aunties and uncles did *not* risk their lives *fightin'* for civil rights so that I could sit next to *Kristin* here whining about not looking like a straw with a *head*. If we'd a known that y'all were gonna talk so *stupid,* we'd a *begged* for *separate* schools."

By fifth grade, Keesha was already no one to be taken lightly.

Anna was the jock. The summer before, Anna had taught Keesha and Kristin to dive in perfect arcs off the high dive at our local community pool. It was so amazing to see someone with the ability to do beautiful, athletic, incredible things with her body and the mastery to teach others how to do it too.

I myself never tried. I said I was scared of the height, but actually I thought that swimming pools were communal toilets. Spas for germs. So even though there was enough chlorine in the water to turn us all into summer blondes, I hung out on the side of the pool, where it was dry and germs would have to travel into my system by air.

My friends didn't push me, though. Our relationships were easy. We knew each other's parents. I even felt comfortable enough to bring up the subject of my fears during a lunchtime conversation about horror movies.

"Freddie Krueger," said Anna while eating her sandwich and spraying us with tiny wads of bologna and spittle. "I had nightmares about those nails!"

"Pffft!" scoffed Keesha. "Nightmares about a creep who needs a manicure? Now, Dracula, he was something to worry about, girl."

"Did anybody see *Interview with the Vampire*?" Kristin asked.

We all screamed happily. "Um . . . I've got something to ask you guys," I said. "And I'm serious, so listen."

Keesha, Anna and Kristin turned toward me. There was a dramatic pause. "Do any of you ever get scared of your own thoughts?" I asked. My friends looked at each other and shrugged silently. It felt as if years went by as I waited for an answer. It was the first time I'd ever admitted that my thoughts scared me.

"No," said Keesha. Then, after another long moment during which my stomach felt as if it was doing a figure eight on a roller coaster, Keesha added, "We always been scared a *your* thoughts."

Everybody laughed. Even me. Keesha put her arm around my neck, kissed my cheek and stole a chocolate chip cookie from my lunch box. Then the bell rang and we had to get ready for my most hated subject—gym. I groaned.

"Come on, Tara, I'll show you how to put on a gymsuit," laughed Anna, and we tumbled out of the cafeteria.

I knew how to put on a gymsuit. In fact, the exertion of putting on my gymsuit was usually the extent of my exercise. I was terrible at gym. When my school picked teams, the jocks picked kids in wheelchairs before me.

But I didn't care. I liked daydreaming and hated running. I didn't want to learn how to dribble or volley or press my own weight.

"Tara! Let's go," screamed Wendy, the captain of our volleyball team. I mumbled something about how stupid it was to have gym after lunch. Then I threatened to hurl, and took my position on the court while sticking my finger down my throat. Almost everybody laughed. Not Wendy, though. She wanted to win.

The ball was served and then, as usual, instead of paying attention to the game, I found myself counting the number of times I heard the ball make contact with the floor, a fist or even the occasional head. I never knew why I was so interested in the sounds of the ball being played, but the thud was pleasant to me. And the game was *boring*. I closed my eyes and inhaled. The gymnasium smelled like sweat, perfume, disinfectant and something sour . . . rotting shoes? I guessed this smell must be an olfactory turn-on to jocks. I wondered if cheerleaders or sponsors of the Olympics had ever tried to bottle it.

"*Tara!*" The ball grazed my ear and fell at my feet, and the other team scored a point and cheered.

I looked at my friends and said, "Ouch."

Wendy went ballistic. "*That's the last time! That's it! What's up with you, Tara! You didn't even try to hit the ball!*" Her face was red with anger. I looked around for our teacher, Miss Susan, who often cut out of our games to smoke outside the building.

"*Giiirrrlll!*" said Keesha, and everyone giggled. I shrugged at Wendy and glanced at Anna, the jock, who looked torn between agreeing with Wendy and being my friend.

"That's it!" screamed Wendy. "I've had it. That was your ball and you were somewhere else in your head again! You're off the team!"

What luck! I'd never dreamed I'd have the good fortune to resume my place on the sidelines with the physically handicapped, who, admittedly, didn't look all that happy about getting me back. "Okay," I said evenly, trying not to show my joy. "Thanks." But Wendy grabbed my arm.

"Not so fast. I gotta know, *why didn't you even try to hit the ball?*"

"Because," I replied, and the gymnasium went silent. "Because, what's the point?" I asked.

"What's the point?" Wendy's eyes were slitted with hatred. *"What's the point?"* I could feel the entire class's eyes on us.

"Yeah. I don't see the point. If I hit it back to them, they'll just hit it back to us. So why not just keep it, as long as they insist on hitting it over here?"

Even though they were on my team, Keesha, Kristin and Anna laughed until they cried. Wendy ran out screaming at everyone and eventually got a note sent home about her bad behavior. Keesha nicknamed me Jordan, after Michael.

I'd always liked daydreaming more than sports, so I didn't feel bad about my gym status. In fact, I would have liked to be more casual about my other schoolwork. But I was as rigid in the classroom as I was easygoing in the gymnasium. If my handwriting wasn't perfect, I'd erase and do it again . . . erase and do it again . . . erase and do it again, until . . .

"Tara?"

"Hhhiiiyyyaaahhh!" I was always so startled when

interrupted that I could have leapt to the ceiling and hung from the tiles. "Sorry. Yes?"

"Everybody else is finished."

"Okay," I said, handing over my test and thinking, *But everybody else's is probably sloppy.*

Although my tests were neat, they were almost never finished, because of how much time it took to make them look perfect or because I really *thought* about the questions. *Really* thought about them. I was in an advanced reading class and the work was challenging. Multiple choice was very time-consuming. As an example:

31. Larry and his friends decided to _____ all modern conveniences and camp out as the pioneers used to.

a. forsake   b. justify   c. belittle   d. exploit

Although I could see that a. was the answer that my teacher was looking for, I couldn't help considering the ramifications of b., c. and even d. I thought of how people regularly *exploited* modern conveniences while *belittling* them and then tried to *justify* doing so. Unfortunately, with all that thinking, I wasn't coloring in enough dots to finish.

"Tara?"

"Hhhiiiyyyaaahhh!" It was a rerun.

"Sorry. Yes?"

"Everybody else is finished."

"Okay."

———

But despite the good things in my life, and for no reason, I began to worry again. Constantly. About everything. I worried so much that I worried about worrying. And I didn't know why. Worries just popped into my head. I'd see a squirrel and imagine it smashed by a car and then I'd imagine other car accidents with smashed and bloody humans. I imagined terrible things happening at home while I was at school and unable to help. My father could die. My mother could die. My sister could run away. And what would I do without them? How would I be able to stand their loss? I knew my worries weren't normal. I knew because my friends had worries too, but they were nothing like mine. Mine were perpetual. And horribly vivid. They came between me and the real world. Also, I had a nagging suspicion that maybe I was responsible for the bad things that were happening in the world . . . like maybe I could be doing something to stop them. I just didn't know what.

To distract and comfort myself, I started to draw large, safe, happy families in the margins of my workbook or test papers. Then I started drawing rope around the families. Instead of just drawing them together, I tied them together. I drew smiles on their faces. My teacher noticed. My grades were starting to slide a little. She wrote a letter to my parents hinting that I might have some attention deficit problems.

"I pay attention!" I hollered at my mother. "I pay attention to *lots* of *stuff* . . . *more* than *most* of the kids! I *have* to pay *attention* to all different stuff . . . *at the same time*! I think I have *attention overload*!"

It was true. For as long as I could remember, I'd been an advanced student, able to pay attention to both the world around me and the one in my head. It was like playing two video games at once or watching television and listening to the radio. It was noisy. It was exhausting. It was stressful. It was not attention *deficit*!

My mother clicked off the television program she was half-watching. "Then stop drawing."

I put my head in her lap and smelled detergent and something else . . . perfume? "Okay," I promised. "I will." And then I thought how pleasant it might be to be tied to my mother, how secure it might feel. I wanted the umbilical cord back again. I doubted she'd feel the same if I told her.

"Is there something bothering you?" she asked, so sweetly I almost smelled flowers.

"No!" I lied. "No!"

I didn't tell her I was worried all the time. I didn't want to worry her. Anyway, I didn't like to say my worries out loud.

I did keep my promise to stop drawing pictures in class, though. But right after that, I started to collect troll dolls. Little naked fat people with short legs and long punk hair. I lined seven or eight of them up on my desk and whispered to them in class.

"Pay attention," I'd tell them in a strict voice. "Come on . . . turn around . . . look at me. What are you thinking? Are you happy? Are you thinking that you're naked, with weird hair? Are you worried about falling on the floor, getting stepped on . . . being separated from the others? Well, don't. I'll protect you. I promise."

They made me happy. They never changed. They always looked the same. They were always smiling.

Troll cheer notwithstanding, my worries got worse. By January, school was becoming difficult. For the first time in my educational career, when I looked at the blackboard, I discovered that I didn't understand most of the math problems.

Unfortunately, my perfectly reliable, always smiling troll family couldn't prevent my teacher's expression from changing when she saw that my workbook page was blank.

"All right, Miss Dizzy Dame."

I looked up from my trolls and examined Mrs. Prack's frown lines.

"Huh?"

"If you don't want to participate, you can just go in the closet."

Without so much as a glance at my classmates, I flew into the closet and hugged myself in victory. I was free! I could hear everything that was being said but I didn't have to participate. Mrs. Prack didn't know what to think, but my classmates thought I was funny. I could hear them laughing as I examined their coats, hats and scarves.

Although everyone could see I had a lot of odd behaviors and was gym-challenged, I was still well liked and social. So even though I was disruptive—or maybe because of it—I managed to be popular. More class clown than crackpot. I thought everyone guessed I wanted attention, that I was getting something I needed to compensate for something I was lacking. And I was more than willing to meet them halfway.

During a lecture on drug abuse, I tied all my troll dolls together using an entire container of dental floss that someone had left in the girls' bathroom. I dangled them from my desk.

"Tara!"

"What?"

"Why are your trolls hanging from dental floss?"

"I think they're high on drugs," I said with a straight face.

Everyone laughed. It took Mrs. Prack quite a while to restore order. I repaid her by paying strict attention for the rest of the day. It worked. She liked me, appreciated me, let me be me, even though she didn't quite get me.

My mother was working on her computer when I got home after school. "How was your day, honey?" she chirped.

"Good," I said. "We learned about drug abuse."

"Hmmm. What did you learn?"

"That drugs kill your body. And that lots of people are addicted to drugs. Maybe even people we know. People who need help. Mrs. Prack asked us what we'd do if we found out our parents were addicted to cocaine. Would we call the police to have our parents arrested? Would we talk to our parents? Or what?"

I didn't mention that I had tied up my trolls with dental floss so that they didn't accidentally get separated.

"What did you say to that?"

"I said that I'd call the police and have them talk to you."

My mother burst out laughing. Her reactions are usually unpredictable to me, but I really didn't expect this. "Well, then, honey, let me suggest that you make sure you've got some extra change to call the orphanage where you and your sister will be living after you call the police, okay?"

I was stunned. "Did you ever take drugs?"

My mother held out her arms and I sat on her lap. She kissed my neck. "Not enough for you to be as goofy as you are."

That was not a good answer. I felt sweaty and dizzy. I couldn't catch my breath. "So . . . you took drugs?"

My mother's smile faded. "Come on, honey. I was playing with you. Trying to keep you from worrying about . . ."

"You took . . . drugs?"

"I don't want to talk about this with you yet, honey."

"Why?"

"Because you overreact!" My mother turned off her computer and gently pushed me off her lap. Finally she said, "I smoked pot. Marijuana. I don't regret it. I'm not sorry about it. I don't do it now. I believe that it is less harmful than alcohol, which is bad for you but legal. And someday marijuana may be legal too. Now, that said, it doesn't mean I want you to do it or anything else until—"

"Did Daddy?"

"Ask Daddy."

"I don't want to talk about this!" I ran to my room sobbing. In the comfort of my bed, I said a prayer for my mother. I worried about her drug abuse. I worried about my father as well but was too afraid of the answer to ask him the question. I wondered if my sister and I could end up in an orphanage. I wondered if my mother was secretly addicted to cocaine.

For months after that I monitored my mother's whereabouts. I stayed home from school to supervise her behavior whenever I could fake an illness. I surprised her on the toilet by bursting into the bathroom after her. I snuck up on her in the laundry room while she was doing permanent press. I even followed her into the pantry to make sure she wasn't smoking or snorting or popping pills. When she started locking doors behind her, especially the bathroom door, I began listening in on her phone calls to make sure they weren't with drug dealers.

By February my fears showed on my face . . . and hers. My dark circles got blacker. Her light anger got whiter. My pale skin got thinner. The lines around her mouth got thicker. I looked tired, worried and anxious. She looked tired, worried and anxious. I could have been a poster child for iron supplements. She could have been a premenopausal villain in a fairy tale.

"Is it Halloween again?" sang Keesha one morning as we were taking off our coats and putting them in our lockers. I made a face.

"Leave her alone. She just needs a little blush," said Kristin.

"Blush! She needs full body paint," laughed Anna. "And a nap. Maybe a year of naps." Anna wasn't alone. A lot of people assumed I didn't sleep enough or had bad allergies. Both of which were accurate but not responsible for my scary appearance.

Mrs. Prack and my parents had a lot of conversations about me. They discussed my daydreaming and my odd habits with trolls, volleyballs, basketballs and closets. But because my grades were usually good and I had a lot of friends, they agreed to do nothing and hoped I'd grow out of my worries.

Then, one freezing day in late winter, while waiting for the bell to ring, I heard someone on the playground say, *"Steponacrackbreakyourmother'sback,"* and my entire life changed.

4
Counting

It was as if invisible dictators had snuck into my brain, held my real thoughts hostage and made me a slave to their whims. After days of hearing almost nothing in my head but *steponacrackbreakyourmother'sback* over and over again, I knew they were powerful invisible dictators. No matter how hard I tried, I couldn't not think the monotonous, scary refrain . . . and once I began to count the cracks, I couldn't stop.

I made up excuses about why I couldn't walk to or from school with my friends anymore.

"I gotta leave early/I'm gonna be late/I need to memorize our spelling words/My mom is punishing me/I've given you up for Lent/I'm coming down with a cold and don't want to sneeze on you/You have a cold and I don't want you to sneeze on me/I need some alone time."

They didn't believe me. They were confused. They were mad. Eventually, though, they stopped arguing and left me alone. I missed them. I needed them. But I was too busy being terrorized by the tyrants in my head to give any other feelings or needs much thought.

Counting cracks was horrible, monotonous, embarrassing, unexplainable, isolating and public. Even though I tried to count quietly in my head and as quickly as possible, I knew people were watching me and listening to me. I could feel the pity and wonder on the faces of their parents and baby-sitters. When they looked at me, they saw a girl with her head down, eyes a few feet ahead, mumbling and sometimes crying. I could hear the exchanges as I was counting.

"What's she doin'?"

"Shhh!"

"What's the matter with her?"

"Don't stare; it's not polite."

"But what's she—"

"*Shhh!*"

It was a nightmare and I was awake. It was hell and I was alive. It was unbelievable and yet it was happening. Over and over and over again. In the sunshine, rain and cold. If it snowed and people didn't shovel, I'd have to check with my toe to make sure the crack was there or I'd feel very nervous. The day Mrs. Scott made me stop and talk to her, I had to go all the way home and start again. By the time I got to school, I was twenty minutes late and breathless in my apology.

"I'm sorry, Mrs. Prack." I ran across my classroom and slid into my desk without looking at the faces of my classmates and friends. Kevin threw a spitball at my face and when I looked up he smiled.

I turned to Mrs. Prack. "I forgot my homework and had to run back for it." That was the second lie I remembered telling in my life. The first was to Mrs.

Scott. I didn't want to tell either of them. But I was more afraid to tell the truth than I was of God's punishment.

Keesha sighed really loudly and then whispered, *"Giirrll."* A few kids giggled. Richard and Kevin gave each other a high five. Emily looked smug.

"That's all right, Tara," said Mrs. Prack with a sweet smile. "I haven't said anything yet today that you'll need to know for the rest of your life."

A couple of kids laughed at her joke. But as nice as it sounded to the others, I didn't like it at all. Suddenly I realized that there would come a time when a teacher, maybe this one, would say something I would need to know for the rest of my life. *What if I wasn't listening? What if I wasn't there? What if I missed it?* I was so freaked out that I couldn't look up. It was obvious. There were going to be cracks everywhere I looked from now on. I felt doomed to insane thoughts and vulnerable to knowing that they were insane. How could I be sane and my brain be insane?

That day, even lunch with my friends was hell. Keesha came right out with it. "Awright . . . straight up. Whadzupwitchoo?"

I knew Keesha wasn't as mad as she was pretending to be. I also felt she was trying to make us all laugh, or at least lighten up a little. I opened my mouth but nothing came out. Keesha continued. "An' no b.s.'n'. We want to know why you don't walk with us anymore. And also . . . what you're doin' by your lonely, pale, mumbling self."

I looked from Keesha's kind eyes to Anna's steady gaze and finally settled on Kristin, who looked as nervous as I felt.

"I count," I confessed.

"We all do," said Keesha, with irritation in her voice.

"No, I mean . . . I *really* count."

"You count what?" asked Anna.

"Cracks . . . "

"Cracks?" Kristin looked confused.

"In the . . . sidewalk."

"Why?" they all shouted like a Greek chorus.

I started to cry. I was so embarrassed. My friends looked at me with sympathy but I couldn't tell them that I was counting cracks so that I didn't break my mother's back. By then, I wasn't even sure if that *was* the real reason. I suspected I didn't know the real reason. I ran to the bathroom and threw up.

Later that day Anna asked me if I wanted to keep score for her Little League games. "I just thought that if you like to count . . . why not?"

The *why not* was that I didn't have time. I was too busy counting cracks. I tried to explain but I just started to cry again. It was all so irritating and embarrassing. What a horrible day. Humiliated and agitated beyond belief, I counted the cracks on my way home as fast as I could. I just wanted to get the day over with. I resented having to count the cracks at all, but the urge was always more powerful than I was. Before I knew it, I was home.

"Tara, is that you?" my mother asked with a certain edge in her voice.

"Uh-huh." Uh-oh.

"Come in here, honey, I want to talk to you."

I walked into the kitchen, where she was making soup. I looked at the carrots she had chopped and felt sad. Dead wads of orange in complete disarray on the brown, gouged chopping board. Like little redheads after the guillotine. I mourned the vitamin-rich innocence that condemned them to this state of servitude to humans. Unconsciously I began to rearrange them into their original uncut positions.

"What the hell happened with Mrs. Scott?" My mother was not one to mince words—even swear words.

"Don't say *Mrs.*," I said weakly. I was echoing my mother's ongoing joke. Whenever anyone swore, she'd scold them, but not for the swear word.

She didn't laugh. She just waited silently for my explanation. I couldn't tell her. I couldn't burden her with something I didn't understand. I was still shaky after telling my friends about it. And I knew that my mother had been tense since discovering me going through her garbage looking for cocaine mirrors or heroin needles. "Nothing," I said.

"That's exactly what she said. No hello. No answer to her call. No idea which way school is. What's going on?"

"I was walking along . . ." I stopped to examine the carrot pattern on the chopping board. Instinctively, or maybe knowingly, my mother put her hand on top of mine and messed them all up again. I felt queasy.

"And . . ." my mother prompted.

"*And* I was thinking my thoughts when I realized that I forgot my homework! So I didn't hear her when she called me at first and then I came home to get my . . . homework. . . ."

"But I was here," she said. "You didn't come back." This is the problem with not being a latchkey kid.

For the first time, I wished my mother worked in an office instead of as a freelance writer in our house.

"Well?" she asked.

"Well, I didn't come all the way back because I checked my bag when I got to our porch and realized that I had it after all," I said. I was lying like crazy that day and getting used to it too. I checked my nose to see if it felt longer.

My mother put her hand on my shoulder. "Mrs. Scott hinted that you might be on drugs," she said slowly.

I didn't even exhale. *Drugs!* I was afraid to take vitamins!

"I didn't tell her that you've been trying to have my urine tested for months!" my mother added.

I didn't know what to say.

Suddenly my mother burst out laughing and kissed me. "The nosy, presumptuous busybody. Suggesting that my scared, protective, spaced-out baby is on drugs! I told her I couldn't even get you to take allergy medicine!"

I loved my mother so much. She loved me, trusted me and was always eager to find all sorts of stuff funny. No wonder I went through so much trouble to keep her back unbroken. As soon as she walked out of the kitchen, I straightened the carrots and went to my room to reorganize my underwear drawer. I was very neat and getting neater all the time.

And keeping me company while I was straightening the carrots, reorganizing my drawer, eating dinner, doing my homework, talking to Keesha on the phone, brushing my teeth, kissing my parents good night and falling asleep was the continual sound track in my mind of: *Step on a crack, break your mother's back!* over and over and over and over and over and over and over and over and over and over. I thought I must be going nuts.

5

Impure Thoughts

Keesha and I were the only Catholic kids in my class who went to catechism classes. We'd been walking to and from St. Francis together on Wednesday afternoons since first grade. We made out first communion together. We planned to take each other's first names as confirmation names. We were sisters in our faith. And even though she said that she, Kristin and Anna were "afraid a my thoughts," I knew she was kidding. She never minded my doubts and consistently reassured me that I was not going to hell. She did mind that I tried not to walk to catechism class with her anymore, though. She minded that a lot.

"So . . . *Count* Taracula . . . you ready?" she asked, handing me my jacket.

"Can't you just walk by yourself?" I begged. *"Please."*

She smiled and shook her head. "Nope. I can't."

"Why?" I begged.

"I don't know why. I just can't. Maybe I'm scared."

"No, you're not," I said. "You're making fun of me, and that isn't very nice!"

"Prove it," she said with a sickeningly sweet smile.

"Dammit!" I swore out loud for the first time. And I was going to have to go to confession for swearing *and she knew it*.

"Don't go cussing at me. It's not my fault you'd rather count cracks than talk with me."

I had an impure thought. *Keesha is an asshole*. And then I had another one for no reason that I could think of. *Sister Margaret is an asshole*. And then I had an unthinkable impure thought: *God is an . . .* I instantly broke out in a cold sweat.

"Tara?" I heard Keesha's voice, but it seemed far away.

I was freaked out. Where did such terrible ideas come from? Did they come from God? Was God sending me terrible thoughts about Him? In tears I turned on my heels, away from our catechism class, and ran toward the church. I had a lot to confess.

Saving Souls

To compensate for my new and frustrating sinful thoughts, I studied my catechism with a God-fearing piousness and memorized details about the fabulously self-mutilating saints. I scratched my eczema and waited for my calling to the convent from God. It never came. The only voice I heard in my head was my own, and it usually said: *Step on a crack, break your mother's back.*

Spiritually frustrated but energetic, I decided to save as many souls as I could in my own small way. From that moment on, anytime anyone swore or took the Lord's name in vain, I said a prayer for their soul and punctuated my plea with the sign of the cross.

My family found my new quirk very irritating. Actually, my father tolerated it as another in my series of what he referred to as stages. My mother wasn't so philosophical. And after a few months of it, she was pretty hostile whenever she saw me do it.

Like the time she kicked the car door shut because she had groceries in both arms and got her skirt stuck in the door. "Son of a bitch already!" she said in frustration. I instantly came to her aid.

"Our Father who art in heaven, hallowed by thy name . . ."

"Cut it out!" she warned in a very sharp voice. And then she said, "Dammit."

"Don't say 'it,' " my sister, Greta, said hopefully, trying to deflect what she knew was coming.

"Okay," my mother said emphatically. "Damn!"

I said another prayer. This time it was silent. But she saw me make the sign of the cross.

"I'm warning you," she said, with murderous eyes.

I nodded, but I knew I would pray for her soul the first chance I got, which was right away.

Unpacking the groceries and already agitated, my mother caught me murmuring a Hail Mary.

"Cut it out, Tara. *Please,*" she begged.

But I couldn't. *". . . and blessed is the fruit of thy womb . . ."* I made the sign of the cross.

She swatted a dishtowel toward my face. *"Cut it out, I said!"*

I cut it out. Not because she asked me to but because I was finished. Satisfied, I began putting away the canned goods. Then I noticed that my mother had seated herself at the table, in the midst of a lot of groceries, and was doing nothing. I stopped and looked at her.

"If I see you doing that one more time," she said without looking at me, "I'm going to punish you . . . severely . . . *Goddammit!*"

By the time she said "God," I was halfway through the sign of the cross and muttering an Our Father.

My mother was swearing like a marine and washing down aspirin with warm beer that we had just bought for a barbecue.

One day she pushed me up against the wall and pinned my hands at my sides. Her face, inches from mine, was a mask of terror, anger and hate. "Do you do this at school? Do you? Do the kids make fun of you? They do, don't they? They'd have to."

I closed my eyes and mumbled a prayer for my poor mother's anguish. When she saw my lips moving, she put her head on my shoulder and whispered in my ear, "I'm going to kill you if you don't stop this." At that moment, my father happened to walk into the room and pulled her off me. Her face was red and she was fighting tears as she fell into his arms.

"You're grounded!" she screamed at me. "Now get the hell out of here."

Did she have to say "hell"?

I crept off to my bedroom, threw myself on my bed and prayed for her. Then I repeated the prayers again and again as I listened to my parents fighting about me.

"She's nuts!" my mother screamed. "And all that catechism is what's doing it to her."

"I don't know," said my father. "You're not Catholic, and I couldn't vouch for your sanity right now."

As I finished a last prayer, my little sister came into my room. She had been standing in the doorway waiting for me to finish praying. She crawled into my bed next to me and looked into my eyes in this eerie, unblinking way of hers that made me think she saw into my soul, into my heart, into my pain.

"Am I nuts?" I asked her.

"I don't know," she answered without blinking. I felt chilled. Even *she* thought I might be nuts. I briefly wondered if it was my mother's fault. If I acted like this because she had smoked marijuana before I was born.

41

After the chill of that fear passed, I realized how ridiculous the thought was, and for some reason, unlike so many other ridiculous fears, I was able to dismiss it.

"I'm grounded again," I said.

She shrugged.

I continued. "She'll never stick to it, though. She thinks I'm home too much as it is. Yesterday she told me if I watched any more television I'd grow a satellite dish out of my forehead."

My sister burst out laughing. I loved it when she laughed. I loved her. A silent, messy little child, she lived in her head as much as I did in mine, except she seemed not to care. My mother's voice came through the walls like a wail.

"Do you think it's our fault?"

"I don't know," my dad answered.

"I could take the nightmares, the weird behavior and the fears . . . but I can't take this praying shit! I really can't . . . I can't . . ." My mother's voice trailed off into sobs.

"So, you can't control yourself either?" It was a direct challenge.

"I'm afraid of what it'll do to her. I'm afraid she'll start seeing herself as . . . a nut."

"If *you* keep calling her one, I don't see how she can escape that feeling," he answered.

My mother started sobbing. My father's tone changed. "It's a stage," he said. "She'll get over it."

"Will she?" she asked hopefully.

After a long silence, my father spoke. I could barely hear him. "Do *you* think it's our fault?" he whispered. His anguished voice sent shock waves through the house. Something fell. There were footsteps. A door slammed. And then it was quiet. Too quiet. I felt sick. I shut my eyes and prayed. My sister hugged my arm. Suddenly pain ripped through my abdomen. I pulled my legs up and lay in the fetal position. I was afraid of the pain and afraid of acknowledging the pain.

"What?" my sister asked.

"My stomach hurts," I said.

"Maybe it's just your nerves again," she said.

I didn't know. I was afraid. "I'm afraid they'll get divorced because of me," I croaked.

"Nah," she said quietly. "As long as they've got you to think about, they don't have to think about other stuff."

Something crashed to the floor in my parents' room. I started to pray.

"Want me to beat 'em both up for you?" Greta asked. We both cracked up laughing. Then I finished my prayers, which included a prayer for Greta. I hadn't walked to or from school with her either, and she never complained. Maybe she didn't want to walk with me. I thanked God.

A few days later, my parents sent me to the family internist, who poked me everywhere. I had enemas, X rays and more poking. Baffled, the doctor sent me to a specialist. The specialist couldn't find anything wrong with me either. He suggested I see a shrink. Odd when you think about it. I'd been counting cracks for almost a year, but it was the praying that I couldn't conceal and that couldn't be tolerated.

The psychiatric evaluation was painless. I didn't even know the guy was a psychiatrist. I thought he was a

43

guidance counselor with a bad wig and long fingernails. His office was neat and I liked that. But his nose was crooked and I didn't like that. It was also too long, so I suspected that he was like Pinocchio and told lies.

"What are you thinking, Tara?"

"I'm . . . I'm thinking about . . . Pinocchio."

"Do you like marionettes?"

"No."

"Do you feel like someone is pulling your strings?"

I had to think about that one, but I didn't really have an answer. Some *one*? *Like God or the Devil?* "I don't think so."

"What do *you* feel like talking about, Tara? Right now."

"I feel like . . ." I concentrated on his nose. "I feel like lying about something. Right now."

In addition to that Pinocchio conversation, we played games, looked at pictures and talked about my family, my fears, the fire drills and the troll dolls. He asked me to finish the sentence "People think I'm . . ."

I told him I really didn't know for sure what other people thought.

"Okay," he said. "What do you think you are?"

"Hmmm . . . odd, I guess."

"Odd? That's it?" he asked while trying to wiggle a piece of dirt out from under his fingernail with a paper clip.

"Isn't odd enough for you?" I asked.

He thought about it. "Yes," he finally admitted. "One more question. Please finish the following sentence. 'I am scared of . . .' "

"Being," I answered. The dirt wedge flew from under

his fingernail and landed somewhere in the carpet. It made me kind of sick.

The meeting with the shrink ended, and aside from the revolting black fingernail trajectory, it hadn't been all that unpleasant.

Diagnosis: Insecurities and self-esteem problems.

Because my mother and father were ambivalent about the experience and fearful of being found insufficient as parents, it was the first and last time I ever saw that doctor, though I thought about his fingernail *schmutz* for a long time.

7
Bullies, Greta
and Friendship

I knew if I tried to control the praying by making a huge effort to pray *inside* my head most of the time, my parents would continue to try to act as if I was normal, and the memory of the shrink's diagnosis would fade. During the summer between fifth and sixth grade, my life seemed to return to almost normal. I still counted and prayed and worried about stuff, but I also went to summer school at the museum, hung out with Keesha, Anna and Kristin and enjoyed sleepovers, movies and a lot of Ben & Jerry's ice cream.

I never *went* anywhere with my friends, though. I always met them at our destination so that I was free to count as much or as little as I needed.

In the fall, when I started sixth grade, I left home very early so that I could avoid people I knew while counting the cracks. After school, however, it was nearly impossible not to be noticed. Even though my friends had become tolerant of my counting, my worries and my fears, I was constantly at risk for ridicule.

Not long after school started, a new girl in my class stepped into my path on the way home and began to make fun of me because of the way I walked with my head down counting the cracks. I say "began" because before she could enjoy her own performance, my sister appeared from out of nowhere, punched her in the face, knocked her down and sat on her stomach. "You still interested in how she walks? You? Who can't even get up? Come on. Say something . . . say anything about her ever again . . . *I want to kill you.* I really do." Two years younger and thirty years tougher, with a lot of unused hostility, my sister might not have had much to say, but when she talked to people they generally listened. Afterward, when the principal called her into his office and told her she would be suspended, she replied sweetly, "Cool," and felt she had been rewarded for her loyalty.

My parents didn't see her suspension as a reward, but they didn't punish her for it.

The second, and more life-altering, incident was with Paulo, the bad boy at my school who followed me down the street with some of his friends. I knew they had been behind me for blocks but I just kept my head down and kept counting.

"Say, Jordan . . . Michael Jordan, whatcha countin', Jordan? I know it's not baskets."

"Leave me alone!" I blurted out. I was instantly furious with myself for the interruption from my counting but I didn't lose count and I didn't go back.

"I heard you've got . . . *urges,*" he said, so menacingly that my blood turned to ice. I was mute. I lost count. I stopped walking. He pushed me into the mouth of an alley and I fell against a garage door. "I've got urges too," he said. A couple of his friends stood behind him and laughed.

I didn't try to defend myself. Instead of screaming or

running, I just stood there, terrified. Paulo put an arm around my neck and grabbed at my crotch while the other boys watched. I twisted my body out of his grasp and fell to the ground.

"Uh-oh! You're clumsy, Tara," Paulo said, smirking. "You're nuts and you're clumsy."

I was mortified. I got up and ran home without counting. I figured that the bad thing for that day had already happened, so my mother would probably be safe from a broken back.

At home there was a note from my mom that she had gone to see my grandma, who was having bladder surgery. I sat home alone and cried until my sister got home from Girl Scouts.

"Want me to beat him up for you?" she asked casually. She put a cold, wet washcloth on my forehead. It seemed funny: Greta standing there in a Girl Scout uniform giving me a compress and asking me whether I wanted her to beat someone up.

"Is . . . there a . . . badge for that?" I asked between gasps for breath.

"Probably."

She was wearing a mobile cast on her arm because of a Rollerblade accident.

"How about your . . . arm?" I asked.

She looked at the cast, looked at me and smiled. "It's no big deal."

The next day Greta walked to school with me. I was counting like mad, partly to protect her. She was silent, as usual. When we got to the playground, Paulo was standing near the sidewalk with a group of boys, including the two who had witnessed what he did to me.

My little sister didn't let a second go by. She walked

up to Paulo and said, "You got a problem?" Then, without waiting for an answer, she slapped him in the face. Real hard.

Teachers would have paid money to see confusion replace Paulo's normally cocky expression.

"I heard you like putting your hands where they don't belong," she said. Actually, it was more like, "I"—*slap*—"heard"—*slap*—"you like putting"—*slap-slap*—"your hands where they"—*slapslap*—"don't belong." *Punch*.

"Hey!" he said. "I'm not fighting a fourth-grade *girl* wearin' a *cast*!"

"Oh," she sighed, "don't let this bother you." And as fast as lightning, she peeled back the Velcro, removed the soft cast with the metal stays and hit Paulo in the face with it. Before Paulo could respond, she jumped on his back and started punching him. Everyone was laughing, mostly Paulo's friends.

In seconds Paulo and Greta were on the ground. Within a minute Paulo's face was bruised and bleeding and Greta had a little scratch on her leg. Although Paulo never shed a tear, Greta had done some serious emotional damage.

She dismounted her victim like a warrior-heroine and bent down to look him in the face. "If you look at my sister again, I'll get our *baby* sister to *kill* you."

Her performance was brilliant down to her exit line. We didn't even have a baby sister! People stopped laughing at Paulo and started cheering for Greta. Keesha, Anna, Kristin and I made a nest out of our hands and threw her in the air a few times to celebrate her victory as she was putting the temporary cast back on her arm.

I read about this Italian dictator who said that it's better to live one day as a lion than a hundred days as a lamb. Greta was a lion. And not just that day.

Greta and Paulo were both suspended. And Greta's arm took more time to heal than it would have if she hadn't taken off the cast and beat up Paulo. But it was clearly worth it.

Both their reputations were changed forever. As a result, Paulo transferred to another school the next year. The rumor was that he had become a ballerina.

Greta, on the other hand, found her place in the sun. If she had to take a back seat to my quirks at home, she was definitely in the driver's seat on the outside. If I was a slave to my thoughts, she was a master of the universe. If I was a victim of my quirks, she was a victor over bullies and evil.

So even with my problems, life seemed good. My parents still loved me. My sister was willing to fight for me. And my friends were loyal to me. With all that incentive, I tried to fight my quirks as best I could. And I stayed very, very busy.

Because I didn't like being away from home too much, Keesha, Anna and Kristin came to my house after school once or twice a week, and usually they'd stay for dinner and after. We'd look through magazines and talk for hours.

"Ohhh! Look! She's so beautiful," groaned Kristin while examining a model wearing more makeup than clothes.

Keesha grabbed the magazine out of Kristin's hands. "She look like she been starved and beaten about the head."

"She does not!" Kristin grabbed the magazine back and touched the glossy page lovingly.

"Then how come her eyes are so black?" Keesha responded. "She's been battered."

Anna and I laughed. Kristin didn't.

"She's beautiful and you know it," moaned Kristin, who was every bit as beautiful, without the black eyes.

"Why?" mocked Keesha. "Why do you think starved, skinny and bruised-lookin' is beautiful?"

"Forget it!" Kristin was sulking. "You don't get it and I can tell you never will."

"Actually," Anna said seriously, "neither do I. I mean, so what if she's beautiful? What is she beautiful *for*? For someone else to look at? What's the point?"

"That *is* the point!" said Kristin defensively. "Beauty is the point. What's wrong with that?"

"She hun-gry! That's what's wrong with that," said Keesha. And we all laughed, except for Kristin, who was on a diet.

"Maybe they're not hungry," Kristin said. "Or just a little hungry."

"But again," said Anna, "why do it? Why be hungry so that somebody else can take pleasure in looking at you? Why deprive yourself of anything so that someone else will like you better? I mean, what do those models get in exchange for their discomfort?"

"Victimized and probably hospitalized, but what the hell," said Keesha. "They're *thiinnn*!"

"Oh, come on! They get to feel special. I'd *die* to be a model," said Kristin.

"Well, I'm special because I'm alive," said Keesha. "And I don't have to do anything special to feel it . . .

least of all starve myself and paint bruises around my eyes."

"Laugh now, but when I'm rich and famous and—"

"—hungry and tired and married to your seventh husband . . ." Keesha had gone too far and she knew it as soon as she saw the color drain out of Kristin's face. Kristin's mom is married to her third husband.

"I'm sorry, Kristin. I really didn't . . ." Keesha was hugging Kristin.

"That's okay. I don't think I'm getting married." Kristin brightened. "After all, I've been to enough weddings . . . mostly Mom's!" We all laughed, and I felt happy that she had made her first joke about something that made her sad.

"Hey, let's make a pact," I said. "Let's never get divorced."

"Unless we want to," said Kristin, and we all shook hands.

"What kind of a pact is that?" asked Anna.

"The flexible kind," said Keesha. We all licked our thumbs and pressed them against each other's thumbs.

"Saliva sisters," I said, laughing.

"Hey, it's safer than mixing blood," said Anna, and we all agreed. Then we lay back down on the floor and picked up our magazines again.

"Think I could model?" I asked while puckering my lips goofily.

"If you were thinner," said Kristin seriously.

"I'm already thin!" I hollered.

"Not thin enough to model," she said matter-of-factly.

"How come white girls think they have to weigh less to be more?" Keesha asked.

The three of us *white girls* shrugged.

"No wonder you all don't do as good in math as the boys," said Keesha, laughing. "Less is not more!"

Kristin was unconvinced. "Don't you ever feel unsure . . . about your opinions, Keesha?"

"I do," I volunteered.

"We know you do!" they said in unison.

"You're unsure you're sitting here!" said Anna.

We all laughed and kicked each other. Then Keesha looked at Kristin seriously. "I feel unsure sometimes too . . . but I know one thing for sure . . ."

We looked at Keesha, who had paused on purpose to get our attention.

"I know that no matter what I do with my life . . . I'm probably gonna do it as a *fat woman*. And I refuse to feel bad about it, now or then. My mama's got a beautiful big butt and I'm probably gonna have an even bigger one! And if I do . . . if I do . . . I'm gonna honor it as a family tradition!"

"No matter what I do, people are probably going to think I'm gay because I'm a jock and not interested in makeup or magazines," said Anna.

"No matter what I do, people will probably think I'm an airhead because I'm blond and pretty," said Kristin seriously.

Keesha rolled on the floor and kicked her feet in the air while imitating Kristin's voice. *"Ohhh! Poor blond beautiful empty-headed me! I'm so mistreated by the world, and it has nothing to do with the stupid-ass things I say about myself like I'm blond and pretty . . . or the fact that you have to starve yourself in order to feel special and would die in exchange for a magazine cover . . . I repeat . . . you'd choose to be dead so that a lot of* other people who are alive could look at you and maybe even think you're pretty. . . . Now, why would anyone think you're stupid?"

Because I'd been quiet for too long, all eyes turned toward me. I wasn't laughing. I was busy counting Kate Moss's eyelashes.

"Twenty-four . . . twenty-five," I said, and waved them off.

Kristin went back to the magazine in her hand. "And no matter what Tara does, she'll do it more than once."

Anna and Kristin shrugged. My friends tried to ignore my quirks, since they didn't have a clue what to do about them. It didn't seem hard on them, though. They were already trained to ignore their parents' alcohol abuse, constant bickering, serial marriages and nonsensical advice.

Stalking My Parents

Trying to control my thoughts, my worries, my prayers and my counting was exhausting. It was like paying attention to a dozen things at once. I was tired all the time. As a result, I got more anxious. I prayed more nervously. I counted with a vengeance.

My parents fought about me all the time. Although they both wanted to help, they didn't know how, or even what was wrong with me. They got increasingly frustrated. They blamed each other by taking turns initiating and ending the following dialogue:

"We should do something."

"What?"

"I don't know."

As time passed, they released their anxiety by fighting about money, movies, friends, the news. I think they eventually got bored arguing with each other, because after a few months they both started to look for reasons to not be at home.

My father turned his care, nurturing and attention toward the American Legion. He'd been a member for years, but it wasn't until he felt the need to "do something" that he turned the Legion headquarters from a decaying money pit into a community center filled with life, laughter and piles of cash.

I hated the Legion. I hated having him gone all the time. I hated feeling as if I had to compete with that stupid building and those stupid events for his attention. But I liked going there with him. And I really liked leaving with him. Because after we'd washed all the glasses, my dad would carefully lock the Legion doors and take me to lunch at the Cavaccios' beef stand. We'd order beef/sausage combos, dipped in gravy with hot *gardiniera*, sweet peppers and lots of salt. Then, standing side by side, gravy running down our arms and the comfort of spicy meat in our mouths, we felt a wave of peace that no amount of conversation could bring. It was comfort, jump-started by smelling, chewing and just being together. It lasted about fifteen minutes, every week. Our happiest times together.

During this same period, my mother took a part-time job as a saleswoman in a department store. An odd choice for a woman who wasn't particularly interested in fashion, but maybe that showed how desperately she wanted to get out of the house. Afterward, however, when the store was closed and locked for the night, instead of coming home to my sister and me, she'd go to the American Legion to meet my dad and socialize for an hour or so. I continually visualized my mother and father in terrible car accidents or being mugged and killed. I could see them lying in pools of their own blood and was terrified every moment they were gone.

To keep them safe, I developed a new ritual and performed it until my anxiety subsided. It wasn't planned. Like the others, it just popped into my head and stuck there. Unfortunately, it was a very odd, obvious and humiliating one.

Aching with embarrassment, I dialed the telephone. The phone rang and rang and rang. I considered the rings a personal rejection. *Pick up! Pick up!* Finally, on the ninth ring, a voice I knew barked into the receiver.

"Legion!"

"Hi, Mr. Spivac. Um, this is Martin's daughter Tara. Can you page either my father or my mother?"

"*Sulliivaaann!* Your *stalker* is calling again!" Actually, he pronounced it STAW-ker. I waited for what seemed like forever, hating Mr. Spivac and listening to the rest of my father's friends laughing at me in the background. Finally I heard my father's irritated voice.

"*What now, Tara?*"

"I'm scared."

"Of what?"

"I don't know."

"What do you want me to do?"

"Come home."

"I already told you I'd be home later on."

"When exactly?"

This went on and on, sometimes four calls in two hours. Both of my parents were patient. But they were mostly glad to be out of the house. No matter how many times I called, I hung up with a lump in my throat and walked down the hallway to my parents' room. I said a prayer to the Virgin Mary plaque that my dad kept on his dresser.

Remember, O most gracious Virgin Mary,
that never was it known that anyone who
fled to Thy protection, implored Thy help,

and sought Thy intercession was left un-aided. Inspired with this confidence, I fly unto Thee, O Virgin of Virgins, my Mother! To Thee I come; before Thee I stand, sinful and sorrowful. O Mother of the Word incar-nate! Despise not my petitions, but, in Thy mercy, hear and answer me. Amen.

I'd say it five times. Every word perfectly pro-nounced. Then I'd carefully set the prayer plaque back on the dresser, walk back down the hallway to the kitchen and stand directly in front of the clock on the stove. *Directly in front of it.* And read the time. From there I'd walk to the living room and stand directly in front of another clock. *Directly* in front of it, and read the time. Then I headed for the front door.

First I'd turn the doorknob carefully with all ten fingers . . . equal pressure on each one. Then I'd walk down the front steps, across the lawn and into the middle—the very middle—of the street. Sometimes it'd take me a while to make sure I was exactly in the middle. Then, when I was satisfied that I was balanced, I'd look both ways twice. Left and then right and then right and then left. Then I'd go back inside. If I was still nervous, I'd start over. Prayer, clock, clock, street. If anyone interrupted me, a neighbor, my sister, a car, I was enraged, because I'd have to start over.

That inner rage was always a surprise and scared me the most. I didn't know I had it in me, and only saw it when I was being thwarted from completing a ritual. Part of it was the frustration of having to do the ritual again, but there was more that I couldn't justify as annoyance. One night even the ritual couldn't help, and in a state of anxiety, I woke up my sister.

"They're not home yet!"

"Huh?" she said sleepily.

"Mom and Dad. They're not home yet!"

"Are you sick?"

"No."

"Then go to sleep."

"I can't! They're not home yet!"

"So?"

She didn't understand. "Can I sleep with you?" I whined.

"If you *have* to."

I had to. Just like I had to count the cracks and say the prayers and look at the clocks from just the right angles and stand in the street looking both ways so that I was even. I had to. But it didn't help.

Lying next to my sister's little body and listening to the regular rhythm of her breathing, I felt fear rush through my veins like hot snakes. Why couldn't I be like her? Why was she sleeping peacefully when I was in agony? She was probably dreaming of something beautiful. *I* was picturing our parents dead. I could see the policeman and social workers coming to tell us. I saw myself fall apart.

Greta felt my anxiety. "It's okay," she whispered. But it wasn't. Waiting was agony. I felt as if my skin was on too tight. Then the urge overtook me.

"I'll be back," I whispered.

I dialed the number and asked Mr. Spivac to page my mother.

"But when are you coming home?" I whined.

"*Schoon,* honey. *Schoon.* Go to bed."

"Are you drunk!" I demanded.

"A little," she admitted with a giggle.

I was furious. "I can't go to bed!"

"Right. Well, honey, *shouldn't* you be *usching* this time to smoke cigarettes, have boys over, be bad for once?"

"Can I talk to Daddy?"

"No."

"Can I call you back in a half hour if you're not home yet?"

A long pause. Finally, "If you want to."

"I don't *want* to! I *have* to!" I shouted. I hung up and headed for my parents' room. I cried lightly while saying my prayers to the Virgin Mary, checking the clock and touching the doorknob. Actually, it was more like whimpering while checking the clock and touching the doorknob.

When I stood in the middle of the street I saw Mrs. McQuade looking out her window at me. I was vexed beyond belief. Didn't she have a life?

I continued with my ritual, ignoring her as best I could. But I felt her watching me. She knew this wasn't normal behavior. I knew she knew. She knew I knew. I didn't want her to tell my parents. So far, they didn't know about this quirk. Now I wouldn't be able to spare them this either.

My heart was pounding with shame and fear. My chest started to hurt. I wondered if it was my lungs that were the trouble all along. Panting with anxiety, I ran into my sister's bedroom again.

"Wake up!"

"What's wrong now?" she asked. Her sleepiness was dulling the irritation in her voice.

"Mom and Dad are still not home!" I was exploding with emotion.

"So?"

"It's after midnight."

"So?"

"I'm—I'm worried!"

"Are you sick?"

"Yes!" I said. "I'm panting."

"That's because you're running another one of your midnight Cinderella marathons."

"So?"

"You're not sick."

"I'm scared."

"Come here. Go to sleep."

"I can't!"

"Then get out of here and leave me alone."

She was maddening. I turned on the bedroom light and sat on her bed.

"Shut that light off."

I ignored her command.

She squinted at me. "Maybe you are nuts."

"It sure looks that way," I admitted.

"Just go to sleep."

"I can't! Not until they get home. Do you think they're all right?"

"They're a lot more all right than you're going to be if you don't get out of here!" Greta staggered out of bed and looked at me menacingly. "I'm getting really sick of this, Tara. We all are. Now shut off that light and get out . . . *okay?*"

"Okay. I'm sorry."

"It's okay. I'm sorry too. But get out now."

I did. And then I did my ritual five more times. All of it. Prayer-clock-clock-street. Prayer-clock-clock-street. Prayer-clock-clock-street. Prayer-clock-clock-street. Prayer-clock-clock-street. Until I saw their car turning the corner onto our street. Then I ducked back into the house and lay in my bed, pretending to be asleep. Pretending to be normal. Scared to death because I wasn't either. Knowing they knew it too. The phone screamed like a siren. It's never good news when the phone rings late at night.

"Hello." My mother's voice sounded tired. "She did *what* in the middle of the *schtreet* . . . street? Tonight? Hmmm."

I was sent to another psychiatrist for an evaluation—a woman whose teeth were so badly capped that she was storing her last Cobb salad between them. She was very casual, and I don't just mean about flossing. Her desk was untidy, and when I looked closely I could see tiny flaws or rips in her clothes. I suspected she bought them that way at a discount, and I doubted her hygiene was up to par.

"How would you describe yourself, Tara?"

I looked from the spinach in her teeth to an ashtray overflowing with paper clips. "Neat. I'm neat."

I tapped the smooth surface of the leather chair with my right index finger. Then I did it again . . . and again. I felt odd, out of balance. As if I might tip over. So I tapped the smooth surface of the leather chair with my left index finger to balance it out. I realized instantly that even if you balance yourself that way, one side always starts first. So one side always starts second. Therefore, you can never really achieve perfect proportions unless you tap at the same time with equal pressure every time. I thought about walking. Did I always start with my right foot? Did I always raise my right hand? If I did, I wondered whether my left side would wither and come to look like a big beige raisin with eczema.

"Neat as in special or cool?" the shrink asked.

"No. Neat as in orderly. I like things to be neat. Really neat. Actually, *really, really neat.*" I couldn't help looking at a pile of messy papers on the floor behind her for emphasis.

"You mean like tabletops and counters and floors?"

"No. I mean like eyelashes, flower petals and even rice."

"I think we've got a lot of work to do, you and me," she said, in such a controlled monotone I wondered which one of us was odder.

Diagnosis: Attention Deficit Disorder. Immaturity.

7

Scared of Being

By winter of seventh grade, my friends were sick of ignoring my quirks and started ignoring me. I couldn't blame them. I was so wrapped up in myself that I hadn't been much of a friend to them. Kristin was busy being hospitalized for anorexia, where she was actually scouted by a modeling agent and signed right there in her hospital room.

When Keesha heard that, she gave up all hope of ever liking Kristin, or fashion magazines, ever again. Even I didn't have much hope for Kristin's future, though I was sure she'd be rich and famous and happy to be getting a lot of attention for a while.

Anna was playing on a volleyball team that took up all her time. And even though Keesha and I still ate lunch together, it wasn't fun anymore. We missed our old selves. We missed Kristin. And we really missed Anna, who now ate lunch with Wendy, the volleyball captain who hated me. I couldn't help feeling betrayed by a weird fate. And sad. Also, it was a really cold, snowy winter and most of the cracks in the sidewalk were covered, which was not impossible, but irritating, to deal with.

Sometimes I'd just count a crack that was covered because I *remembered it was there*. And then I'd be plagued by doubt. Sometimes I'd have to kick the snow away to be sure. I hated people who didn't shovel their sidewalks.

"Ninety-eight, ninety-nine, a hundred, a hundred and one, a hundred and two . . ."

"Hey, Tara!"

"A hundred and three, a hundred and four . . ."

"Tara! Wait up!"

It was Keesha. "A hundred and five, a hundred and six . . ." Despite the intense cold, I was sweating.

"Tara!" Her voice didn't sound mocking this time. She sounded *angry*.

I got angry too. It felt as if my body fluids were starting to boil. I silently begged God to make her go away. "A hundred and seven, a hundred and eight . . ."

"Taarraa!" She was definitely pissed.

Beads of boiling sweat were snowplowing down my back. "A hundred and nine, a hundred and ten . . ."

"Taaarrraaa!"

She was as stubborn as I was possessed. "A hundred and eleven, a hundred and twelve, a hundred and thirteen, a hundred and fourteen, a hundred and fifteen . . ."

"Ta—"

"What!" My response was furious. I was furious. My heart was beating so fast and so loud that I instinctively grabbed at my chest as I looked up to see my friend Keesha standing before me, frowning.

"Girrll, we are so sick of you!"

"Go away!"

"And if I don't?"

"Please leave me alone, Keesha!" I was amazed at how much I was hating my old friend.

"I don't think so."

"Why, Keesha? Why can't you just leave me alone! Huh?"

Keesha looked at me for a long time. "I did leave you alone. We all did. But you didn't get better. You didn't stop. You're still doin' all your weird shit. And I think it's time to stop."

"You think it's time to stop!" I exploded, and lunged at her with my hands outstretched. I pushed her real hard. She almost fell down. *"I don't care what time* you *think it is!"* I screamed. "Do you think I want to do this! Do you think I like it?"

"You pushed me!"

"Yeah. So what?"

"You're so afraid of being interrupted that you pushed me!"

"I'm not scared of being interrupted, you jerk! I'm . . . I'm scared . . . I'm scared of *being.*" I crumpled into a ball and sat down where I was standing. I sat on a crack. Unevenly.

"Who are you anymore, Tara?"

Tears spilled over my frozen lashes and disappeared across my cheekbones. I had never felt so defeated. "I don't know."

Keesha leaned in toward me, but I held back. "Please," I begged. "Leave me alone."

"Okay." Her face was a mask of resigned sorrow and confusion. "I will." It was almost a whisper. And with that she turned around and started to walk away. "We thought you'd get over this . . ."

We who? Over this! I felt like fainting. Instead, I screamed so loudly that Keesha froze on the spot. "*Well . . . I'm . . . not!* I'm not over it! In fact . . . I don't even know what *it* is!"

"I'm sorry, Tara," Keesha said kindly. "I just miss you. We all do."

"*I miss you too . . . and I-I miss . . . I miss me . . . I miss me!*" The icy sidewalk beneath me felt good in contrast to the heat coming out of my pores. In a fetal position, I rocked myself like a sad baby in a cold white crib. I had no language to describe my pain. I had no company in my pain. I just had pain. Isolating, solitary pain. And loneliness. And humiliation.

Keesha dropped down beside me and held me, cradling my head in her lap. "I'm sorry, Tara. I didn't mean to make you cry! I just wanted to walk to school with you."

I sobbed more loudly.

"Shhh. Hey, girl . . . it's okay. It's gonna be okay," she said softly.

If my eyes hadn't been swollen shut, I still wouldn't have been able to look her in the face. Her kindness dissolved my very last resistance against hysteria. I didn't know if I'd ever be able to walk to school with her or anybody else ever again. I missed the way we all used to be, so badly that I felt sick. But the only thing I could do was wail. Breathless, heartbroken, frightened sobs.

10
Bad to Worse

Between March and June, several horrible things happened almost simultaneously. First and worst was my father's heart attack.

"Is he going to die?" my sister asked in a tiny, hollow voice as we watched our father being taken away in the ambulance with my mother at his side.

Pain ripped through my abdomen, shot through my heart and cut a hole in my life. I felt as if my lungs were filling with a cold, damp, permanent sorrow. I cried and prayed again and again and again and again and again and again. My sister cried too.

I tried to comfort her, but I, of course, was more out of control than she was. "He's not going to die. He's not going to die. He's not going to die. He *can't die*!" I sobbed until I couldn't breathe. Then I lay on the floor next to my sister's bed. I needed to be near someone I loved, but touching would be too much for me. Finally I fell asleep and dreamed that everything was okay.

The next day, we all went to the hospital. White walls, white people, white clothing. A zillion machines. As we walked into my dad's room, his green plaid robe greeted our color-starved eyes. He smiled. We smiled. Powerless, we all tried not to cry. The familiarity of his robe gave us hope. It matched the green monitor checking his heart. Green was his favorite color.

For the first time, we all felt out of control, not just me. And without a game plan or rules, we immediately and instinctively began the sort of ritual of duplicity that accompanies events outside of human control. We all began to smile. We acted as if he was going to be fine. We acted as if everything was going to be fine.

I was so wrapped up in my fear and pain that I lost the shred of interest in my friends that remained. I stopped doing any activities outside our house. I stopped doing my homework. I thought of my father and his defective heart constantly. I slept with my mother at night—on my father's side of the bed—and prayed over and over again. My mother didn't go nuts, though. She was busy relieving her anxiety with a glass of wine or two and crying quietly.

After my father came home from the hospital, I kept dreaming that he was dead. To protect all of us from further harm, I stepped up my ritual of prayer. Although my urge to pray for the soul of anyone who swore had lessened for a time, now it returned with a vengeance. Once again no one could say "damn" in my presence without my crossing myself several times and imploring God to forgive him—or usually *her*, my mother—without punishing us.

My father felt he could use any help he could get and accepted my efforts without comment. But the combined stresses of his physical problems and my mental ones took their toll on my mother. Her natural state of mind had become testy. And when she talked, even about ordinary things like groceries or going to the bank, she usually sounded as if her jaw was wired shut.

I prayed for her. I did it while watching television, while unloading the dishwasher and while reading. Sometimes I didn't even know I was doing it. When my mother saw me making the sign of the cross while baking chocolate chip cookies, she threatened me.

"I've been patient," she said calmly, but her voice and body were edgy with anger. "But from now on, *from now on,* every time I see you make the sign of the cross . . . I'm going to slap you silly . . . *sillier!* So please. *Please.* Take this as a warning and stop it. *Now.*"

"Okay. I'll try," I said.

"Good. Because I'd like everybody in this house to think of me for once. Not you and your *things* or your poor father and his health or your sister either. But me-me-me-me. Please." And then she muttered, *"Dammit."*

Immediately I began praying to save her soul. "In the name of the Father—"

Just as immediately, my mother reached out and slapped my face so hard I thought my head would fall off. It was great! I loved it! Tears of humiliation streamed down my face but I couldn't help smiling. My efforts at saving the souls of my family had taken on a whole new dimension. I was being punished for piety. Surely this must erase some of my part in Christ's suffering. After all, I was suffering too now. My flesh was being injured too. And so, with the renewed vigor of a martyr, I ran out of the room, slamming the door behind me giddily.

Needless to say, my relationship with my mother

became more and more strained. My father joked that her reactions to me were caused by PMS, which he defined as Periodically Mean Syndrome. He said not to worry and told me it would pass.

"I hope she doesn't kill me first," I said as a joke.

"Me too," my dad said, but he didn't sound as if he was joking.

To take our minds off our problems, we decided to go to a carnival together. We should have known better. It was like asking for trouble.

The St. Francis of Rome carnival is a big event in our town. It's like a temporary Santa Monica Pier or Coney Island, I guess. When we got there, things seemed ordinary. The carnival was crowded with the usual neighborhood people. Both my parents met a lot of people they knew and seemed to be enjoying themselves. Greta and I saw kids from school and took turns on the games. Some of us won ugly little stuffed toys.

After about a half hour of pretending we were having more fun than we were, it was time for the rides. Mounting the stairs to the Octopus, I reflexively performed a quick sign of the cross. I didn't even really know that I did it. But my mother did.

She grabbed my arm so violently that I almost fell off the platform. "Do that on the ride and I'm going to kill you." I looked at her crazed expression and saw the fear, futility and helplessness she was raging against.

I could have cried right there, but my sister pushed me up the stairs and into the steel-grated egg in front of us. As the carnival worker strapped Greta and me in, my mother and I locked eyes. There was no doubt that she would try to keep her promise if I crossed myself.

I crossed myself. Not just once but again and again

71

for the duration of the ride. I watched my mother standing on the ground next to my dad, who was shaking his head in disbelief.

"Why, Tara? Why?" was all my sister said, but I didn't answer her. I just kept praying and watching my mother even when we were upside down.

When the ride stopped, I was frightened. I knew it was going to take a lot more than the threat of a life sentence or even the electric chair to keep her from killing me. I was dead girl walking.

She knocked two people off the metal stairway leading to the ride and opened the door of our cage before the surprised carnival worker could get to us. Her face was a mask of rage as she pulled me out by my shirt. Crying, I tripped on the last stair and fell to the ground. In an instant, my mother picked me up by my arms as if I weighed nothing at all. She then grabbed both my shoulders and shook me and shook me and shook me, crying harder than I did the entire time.

The moment itself was an emotional stew. A blur of colored Christmas lights arced between laughing, screaming, smiling people enjoying themselves. The smells of buttery popcorn, sugary cotton candy, salty sweat and icy fear filled my sinuses as the metal taste of embarrassment trickled down my throat. Heightened but fragmented senses of sight, smell and taste vied for attention against a dull backdrop of humiliation and sorrow.

Before I knew it, my mother had released me and was sobbing into my father's chest. I wanted to run to her and stroke her hair and tell her it was only a bad dream. But I knew it wasn't. It had happened. It had happened in front of the whole neighborhood. She looked like the saddest person in the world. I was dizzy. And nauseated. My father and sister looked stricken with confusion and divided loyalty.

That moment was the saddest, lowest one of my life, and my mother's. She was determined to fight for my sanity . . . even if she killed me. And I was as helpless against her rage as I was against the tyrants in my head.

That night I slept on the floor at the side of my parents' bed again. I listened to my mother breathing and muttering to herself in her sleep while my father tossed around. I was sorry I'd made her so crazy. I loved her very much but wasn't showing it in any way she could understand. Or I could understand. I couldn't help myself, though. I really couldn't.

My mother must have felt really guilty about the carnival incident, because in the months that followed she tried very hard to ignore my rituals.

Unfortunately, that didn't help to alleviate my anxiety either. I began to fear the dark. I hated wind and was terrified of being alone. Even the nightly squeak of el trains returning to the end of the line that had once seemed comforting in its rhythmic regularity cut a metal slash through my nervous system. I felt sick but wasn't sure of what.

And so I did what I had always done. I clung tighter and tighter to my mother. I became a ball and chain around her neck. I could sense her reluctance, feel her urge to pull away from me. I didn't care. I clung harder and tighter than ever.

One horrible afternoon, while I was watching my mother smiling at me from her NordicTrack, our separateness hit me like a bolt of lightning. I doubled over with anxiety and tried not to think about puking.

"Are you all right?" She didn't miss a swoosh of her NordicTrack.

I looked up at her expression of passive fortitude and suddenly realized that she could outwardly show me patience, affection, love and concern . . .

"Tara? Are you okay?"

. . . while she was with someone else in her mind. I couldn't control her thoughts, I couldn't be sure that I'd ever really know what they were. That I'd ever known what they were. Was this possible? Did I know her at all? Was it all a facade? Was her fury the only thing that cracked the mask of her personality? Was anger the only emotion I could ever be sure she was feeling? Did she have to be out of control to be authentic? Did everyone?

In an instant, I understood that I had a problem I would never be able to overcome. From then on, I knew I would never be able to fully trust my mother. I suspected she was always thinking things that were different from what she said.

Good morning./*I hate you.*

How was school?/*I'm packing my bags and leaving.*

Don't I get a kiss?/*If you touch me, I'll go mad.*

My heart was beating so fast I could barely breathe. My mother had left her NordicTrack and was holding my head and saying something, but I couldn't concentrate on her words.

My mother, father, sister, friends, teachers—they could all think something about me that they weren't telling me. They could pretend. My mother could be pretending she loved my father. She could run off and leave him, and us. Leave us! I could marry someone someday who didn't love me or who stopped loving me without telling me. Who still smiled at me and ate with me and slept with me. And no matter how much any of us loved anyone else, it would never be enough to ensure that the other person felt the same way. Trust was out of the question.

"Are you okay?" my mother asked.

"I'm kinda . . . dizzy," I said.

"You sure *are*!" She laughed and got back on her NordicTrack. "But at least you're not praying."

Ironically, although I desperately wanted to control and monitor my mother's thoughts, I couldn't control my own thoughts at all. They just jumped into my head and took over.

I needed to be alone. I wanted to be alone. To think. To try not to feel. After months of remora-like proximity, suddenly I couldn't stand to be near my mother. Or my father. And the spring rain scared me. So did wind, convertibles, electric can openers and the color red. I didn't know why. I was totally miserable.

11
Donna

I met Donna, or rather was accosted by her, while walking home from church one rainy Sunday in July.

Trying to stay dry, she was standing underneath a garage frame just inside an alley. I knew who she was. I'd just seen her at Mass. I'd seen her for years. She went to St. Francis School. Like me, she was thirteen and going into eighth grade. She was lovely, with dark hair and darker eyes that were almost always hidden by sunglasses.

I'd heard that she'd had surgery to remove a tumor or something from her eye. Everybody talked about the fact that she was tough enough to have let someone poke a needle into her eye zillions of times. Anyway, in the beginning she wore the sunglasses to protect her eye while it healed, but by now they were a part of her look.

She already had breasts and a bra that performed a function. Boys, men and even some women ogled her as she walked down the street. She was beautiful and muscular but also sort of pissed-off and angry-looking. She was popular and tough and only talked to the coolest kids. I was startled that she spoke to me.

"Hey, Twinkie. Got a match?"

"No. I don't smoke," I said coolly.

"You're supposed to say, 'Yeah, I got a match. Your face and my ass.'" I was so surprised and her reply was so stupid and vulgar that I burst out laughing. She raised one eyebrow. I laughed harder. I even forgot to pray for her. Somehow it sounded more like a prayer than a curse anyway. *My face and your ass.* I watched her as she found some matches in the pocket of her leather coat.

"Never mind," she said, a Kool cigarette hanging out of her thin, pink-painted lips at a provocative angle. "I got one."

"A match?" I ventured.

"No." She struck the match in vain. "An ass." Giddy at this spontaneous meeting of unlike minds, I laughed again before asking her, "Did you call me a . . . Twinkie?"

She eyed me evenly. She hadn't found any of this amusing. Finally she spoke. "Relax."

That was it. I was gone. "Relax! Re-lax! Relaaaax! As if . . ." Tears poured down both my cheeks evenly. "Relax! You don't—as if—as if—as if that were remotely possible for me." I wiped my tears away and took stock of myself. In my giddy glee, I had crouched on the ground next to the garage. Both my feet were planted in a puddle of water. "Look, I'm treading water." I laughed and looked around at the neat rows of garages and garbage cans. "Did you ever realize how neat these alleys are? How clean?" I asked. I looked up into her face. Both the angle and her startled lack of a facade were hysterical. I started laughing again. She was dumbfounded. Her tough-girl attitude was gone and in its place was a kid my age playing with matches. She helped me up.

"Thank you," I said.

"People say you're weird," she said. "They're right."

"Yes, they are," I admitted giddily. "Yes, they are."

She finally lit her cigarette, then inhaled through her mouth and exhaled dramatically in little smoke rings that I spontaneously put my finger through. I was going to say, "Hey, look. I'm wearin' your ring," but I was too afraid she would think I was a lesbian trying to go steady with her or something. She looked at me oddly.

"Sure you don't wanna cigarette?" she asked. She looked strange. If I was afraid of the world, she already half-despised it. I had no idea why.

"No." I thought about it. "I've got enough bad habits."

"So I heard," she said, and I froze at the thought of what people must say about me.

"What? What did you hear?" I croaked.

"I heard that your family outings are almost as bad as mine."

In that sentence I could see the kindness and generosity underneath her tough-girl act. I smiled.

"Why did you call me a Twinkie?"

"We're back on that?"

"Yeah."

"All right. Because you look all blond, packaged and spongy."

I considered whether I should be insulted or not, whether I could muster indignation in my current giddy mood.

"Hey, not in a bad way," she explained. "I mean spongy, like you could bounce back."

"Resilient?" I helped her.

"Whatever."

"Creamy," I said thoughtfully.

"Maybe. But only down deep. On the surface you're a lot of other stuff. Chemicals. Preservatives. Probably rubber."

I burst out laughing. "I'm Tara Sullivan."

"I know. I'm Donna DeLuca."

"I know."

By that time we were walking home together in the rain. Actually, we were kind of running. I was so involved with her that I forgot to count the cracks! That omission would make me anxious later that night, but still, I wouldn't go back.

"How can you smoke after Holy Communion?" I asked.

"What is that? Like a commandment? 'Thou shalt not smoke after receiving the body of Christ?' " She was not nearly as serious as I was about anything.

"You're not old enough, so it's illegal."

"Give me the commandment."

" 'Honor thy father and thy mother'?"

"Hey, if I'm not shooting heroin and getting pregnant from aliens, I'm honoring them more than they deserve." We both laughed and laughed. I wondered what her parents were like that she felt that way about them. My mother slapped me for praying too much and shook the saliva out of me at a carnival, yet I'd do anything to keep her safe.

12
Fun

For the first couple of months after we met, I practically lived at Donna's house. In the process, I discovered that her parents were mostly absent. Donna and her sister, who was never home either, had the entire top floor of an old A-frame to themselves. On hot nights, we used to crawl out the window, sit on the roof and make wishes. I mostly wished that we wouldn't fall down and that my parents were still alive and wouldn't get a divorce. Donna mostly wished for mystical things like world peace and a cool boyfriend with a motorcycle. She knew about my quirks. I told her almost all my crazy thoughts. Even the ones about my mother and God and unbaptized abortions. She didn't seem to mind. In return, I didn't mind that half of her truths were imagined, and I never called her on the lies she told.

Under a beautiful August moon, she turned to me and said, "Twinkie, you keep me outta jail and I'll keep you outta the loony bin."

"Deal!" I said, and then hugged her.

She never stopped smoking when she was with me.

Oddly enough, I began to stop counting and praying when I was with her. Maybe it was because I had real things to worry about, like her smoking and lies. Whatever it was that she did for me, for the next few months, I had *fun*!

In matching orange bikinis, we went to the pool nearly every day to enjoy the attention our budding bodies were creating. Donna's breasts were full, like breasts on a statue of Venus. Mine were on the small side of medium. She swam and dove and splashed in the pool. I sort of held my breath and waded through what I sensed was a giant puddle of germs. Despite the warnings, we were both good at tanning and got really brown, which made our teeth look even whiter. We were beautiful and we knew it.

Donna was like a guy magnet. I lived in her orbit. However, I didn't have to be told not to have sex. Having guys put their tongues in my mouth and contaminate my saliva with theirs didn't hold much appeal for me.

I often hung out with Donna and some guy. A third wheel, to be sure. The only ones who ever seemed to mind were the guys, and they were revolving. A different one each week or month, depending on Donna's whims. I was constant.

I had no idea why. But after all that praying, counting and worrying and my horror at not being able to control my mother's thoughts, it all seemed to stop. I fully expected it to return, but in the meantime, I enjoyed my parole by sitting on the shallow side of the pool and watching Donna and some guy splash each other with chlorinated germs in the deep end.

"Well, well, well, if it isn't the Count."

I looked up to see Keesha and Anna looking down at me.

"Hi!" I said happily, even though I didn't like Keesha's tone.

"Hi? Hi?" said Anna. "You told us you didn't want to go out of the house anymore."

"I didn't! That was true."

"Was?"

"Yeah." I felt defensive and confused. I didn't want to hurt my friends, but I could see it was too late.

"Maybe she meant she didn't want to go out of her house with *us*. Like she didn't want to walk to school with *us* or to catechism with *me*." Keesha's voice was mean.

"That's not it, you guys! Really."

"Well, what is *it*, then?" said Anna.

"It's hard to explain . . . ," I began.

"Don't bother," said Anna, and knocked me into the water. When I got out, they were on the other side of the pool practicing their dives. They didn't even glance at me. When Donna came back, we lay in the sun and she tried to cheer me up.

"Hey, if I were you I'd rather be with me than with them. You've just got good taste is all."

I was silent for a while.

"Donna?" I finally asked.

"Huh?"

"Why do you like to be with me? I mean, I'm kinda odd. And I know it. And you know it. But you're popular. You could hang out with anyone, so why me?"

Donna sat up and seemed to consider my question. "I think you're funny. And smart. And caring. I like the way your trippy brain works. It's interesting. If you want to take weird head trips and leave this planet behind, why should I care? I'd like to be able to get lost in my head the way you do."

———

When school started in September, Donna and I were still inseparable. Although we went to different schools, we got together for homework and gossip at night, shopped all day on Saturdays and spent Sundays with whichever of our families was doing something fun.

Sometimes we took the el into Chicago to shop. It made me feel very sophisticated to be taking the el alone with Donna. We were free from our town, free from our neighbors and free from anyone who knew us. It was exciting.

Once downtown, we were like bright threads sailing through a fabric consisting of thousands of other bodies in motion. We line-danced from store to store, in and out of revolving doors, up and down dozens of escalators. Alone. Unsupervised. Kid heaven.

"Ever hock anything?" Donna asked me.

"What's that?"

"Pinch—shoplift—stea—"

"Shhh!" I covered her mouth with my hand and looked around. When I finally met her eyes again, I must have looked frantic. She laughed. I laughed.

"Forget it," she said. But of course I couldn't forget it. Once I knew she was stealing, I was obsessed with the idea. I'd watch her carefully as she'd casually try a headband on her head and leave it there. Or slip a trinket up her sleeve or into her pocket without ever changing her expression. Then, before I knew it, I was doing it too. Just like that. To see how it felt. To see what happened. Which only proves that if I could steal, anybody can do anything.

I wasn't a very advanced thief. Just lipstick, blush, a tube of mascara. But when we walked out of that store, I was dizzy with excitement. I kept waiting for someone to come out, put handcuffs on my wrists, call my parents and arrange a jury trial. I saw myself crying the mascara, blush and lipstick off my ashamed face on the stand. But nothing happened. No one came. I was free. I was exhilarated. I felt power.

Then I saw a reflection of myself in the store window. I didn't look any different, but I had changed. I was now a thief. Yet it didn't show. What else was I that didn't show? What about all the people behind me? What were they that didn't show? Were they thieves, murderers and child molesters? Or were they hardworking, trustworthy people trying to be good?

I looked at Donna and she knew what I was going to do in an instant.

"No!" she cried out from behind me, but my decision was made. I walked back into the store and up to the security guard at the door.

"Here. It's yours. Or theirs. Lipstick. Blush. Mascara. I *hocked* it. And I've come back for my punishment." Before I knew it, I was sitting in a tiny room with Donna, two policemen who worked for the store and the store manager. They let me go. No arrest. No trial. It was all over in less than fifteen minutes. Less time than it took me to confess my sin to poor, bored Father O'Malley, who I believe was almost glad to hear that I finally had a sin worth confessing.

13
Speechless

For the most part, in eighth grade, I was normal. Or at least I acted *more* normal. I certainly felt more normal. My grades improved. And absence must have made my mother's heart grow fonder, because our relationship had improved dramatically and she seemed genuinely happy during the infrequent times when we were together.

Although the nickname "Count" stayed with me, I rarely counted cracks or prayed anymore. I thought Donna had changed my life. Even my parents had to admit that despite Donna's "wildness," she had proved to be a positive influence on my behavior problems.

Unfortunately, though, with a group of kids from her school whom I didn't like, Donna was in the process of changing herself with occasional drug use, and I was helpless to stop her.

Kristin, Keesha, Anna and I were still tense with each other, but we usually ate lunch together anyway, mostly out of habit. And something about an argument between Anna and Wendy. Anyway, Keesha, Anna and I ate. Kristin mostly played with some celery and looked in a compact mirror. I didn't care too much, though, because I had Donna to look forward to after school, if she wasn't getting high.

By Christmas I had a part in the school play. A small part. Actually, I played a candelabra. All I had to do was hold two unlit candles in the air for an hour while wearing a white sheet draped with a garland, but at the end I had a line: "Merry Christmas to all, and to all a good night."

During the performance, I waited in agony to say my line. For an hour and a half, I stood on the stage watching kids who were born to be accountants, computer analysts and mimes acting their hearts out. Each line was more painful than the last. Parents groaned at their own children's performances. Each blackout resulted in a standing ovation; the audience hoped the play was over.

As I looked across the auditorium at the faces of my parents, my sister, Donna, her family and hundreds of others, I suddenly felt a chill run up my spine. Donna looked odd. Judging from her red eyes and faraway expression, she had obviously smoked something more powerful than Kool cigarettes before the performance. I was worried about her. The night before, she had lain under our Christmas tree and claimed that she was trapped in a yellow tree light.

"At least your world is bright yellow," I'd said. "I've spent years trapped in my head . . . and its contents are a lot less cheerful than that bulb." She'd laughed hysterically. I knew better than to lecture her.

I looked at the audience again. My parents looked hopeful that I'd be able to pull this off. My sister seemed interested in the play. Donna and her parents looked bored. My grandparents looked nervous. Suddenly I remembered a story that my grandma told about when she and my mother did an amateur night together. My grandma played the piano and my mom was supposed to sing. But when the curtain went up, they became paralyzed. My gram missed more notes than she hit and my poor mom couldn't get a breath out, let alone a song. Maybe I inherited all my crazy stuff.

I was hot, my arms ached and I was bored. I looked from Donna's dreamy expression to Kristin's tiny body and nervous twitchy expression. I wondered what her life must be like now that her mother was getting divorced again and she was in a makeup ad that ran in magazines around the world. I had less of a relationship with Kristin than with Anna and Keesha. I felt a stab of longing. I wanted to be in my room with the three of them, looking at magazines. I wondered what they wanted out of life. Then I wondered what I wanted. Then I wondered what other people thought of me as a result of my quirks.

I looked at my music teacher. I knew she thought I was shy. Actually, I usually just wasn't listening.

My parents were hopeful that I was over the worst of whatever it was. I hoped so too.

Suddenly, in the middle of my Christmas play, surrounded by people I had known all my life, I felt completely alone. I got scared. I squeezed my eyes shut and realized that I was afraid of growing up, of going to high school, of getting lost, of not being able to breathe.

I looked from right to left and then from left to right. I did it again. And again. Obeying an urge, I was performing an outlandish ritual, onstage, in front of everyone, and they didn't know it. I hoped. My heart was pounding with anxiety. My arms ached from holding the stupid candles in the air for so long. The tyrants in my head were returning with the force of an army. *Please don't make me have to pray! I don't want my mother to drag me off this stage and kill me here in front of everyone!*

The image of Sisyphus rolling that giant stone uphill for eternity popped into my head. What did he do to deserve that? What did I do to deserve this? This play seemed to be taking an eternity.

Mercifully, the curtain slowly descended behind me on the stage. The play was ending. I was standing alone before the audience. My heart was beating like a snare drum. This was it. My moment in the sun. Or was it the son. Sun. Son. Sun. Son.

The spotlight illuminated me. Sun. The candles looked as if they were lit. Sun! All eyes were on me. Mute and tinsel-laden me. I didn't utter a sound. I couldn't utter a sound. The tyrants in my head forbade it.

I was humiliated. I concentrated hard on not crying. After a moment, my mother stood up and applauded as if she had just seen the best performance of her life. Everyone else followed enthusiastically. I was mortified. Keesha was at my side with her arm around me, giving me silent support. I didn't cry, but for the second time I felt her pity and wanted to get away from it. Luckily, when I came home nobody said anything about the play or my nonperformance. Donna had a date that night with a guy she'd met buying cigarettes at the bowling alley.

14

Warrior Angels

Although Donna and I were totally too old, we spent the afternoon of Christmas Day making angel patterns all over my backyard by lying on our backs in the snow and swooshing our arms and legs. Inhaling frosty air through a giant piece of peppermint stick, I studied the cloud-decorated sky and listened to the crusty *whooshes* of our angel music. With Donna by my side, my family tucked safely inside the house and new forest-green Doc Martens on my feet, I felt almost happy—which made me reflexively nervous.

"Do you believe in God?" I asked Donna while digging my elbows deeper into the snow. I looked at a cloud that changed from a woman's profile into a dragon.

"Oh, you're not gonna start that trip again, are you?"

"What trip?"

"That praying trip?"

"No!" I said quickly. And then, "At least—" But before I could finish my thought Donna chimed in.

" 'I hope not.' " Then she added, "Well, if you do it again, try not to be so *annoying* this time."

"Okay," I said. Then I thought about how much I loved Christmas. I loved the comfort and safety promised by Christ's birth. I loved the trees, the snow angels, "The Little Drummer Boy." I loved midnight Mass with the intense colors and more intense music. I loved the incense and the hope. And then I loved coming home and opening presents, getting as many new clothes as possible. I loved my new Doc Martens. I loved two weeks off school. I loved Donna and my parents and—

"I believe in God," said Donna solemnly. She stood up to check out her angel. Although I couldn't really say why, I was bathed in relief to hear that she believed in God. "And goddesses," she added smugly.

"Which ones?"

"All of them . . . and then some."

I thought about her statement. I imagined Roman and Greek gods and goddesses nailed to alabaster crosses. I imagined singing "O Holy Night" in Latin and Greek, dancing down the aisles of the church. Donna interrupted my reverie by throwing a snowball in my face and laughing hysterically.

"Come on," she commanded. "I need a smoke."

Carefully we stepped between the angels and sat down on the other side of the garage so that my parents couldn't see Donna smoking, even though they knew she did it and could always smell it on her breath. When she'd finally got her cigarette lit in the wind, I watched her inhale a long drag. I thought about how close we'd become in the short time I'd known her. How much she meant to me. How comfortable she made me feel in spite of the risks she was always taking.

"Great boots," she said, looking at my new Docs.

"Thanks."

"Christmas present?"

"Duh!"

"So what are you so quiet about today?" Donna managed to exhale words along with carbon monoxide and a thousand other poisons.

I coughed and shrugged.

"People die from breathing secondary smoke," I said.

Donna looked thoughtful. "Too bad I don't get to pick which ones." We laughed and I went back to cloud-watching, but I knew she was watching my face. "I get nervous when you're quiet for too long. You aren't counting snowflakes or something, are you?"

"No. I'm counting the months I've known you."

She smiled, and in those few seconds she looked like her mother. She hated her mother, but I didn't really know why. Part of me thought she hated her mother because she was afraid that if she didn't hate her she too might end up married to someone named Hal and taking medicine for bouts of depression.

"I'm also worried about you taking drugs."

Donna didn't respond. The wind picked up and we shivered.

"I don't complain when you leave the planet behind, do I?" she asked, and I thought about how she saw it.

"Did you really let a doctor poke a needle into your eye zillions of times?"

She looked startled. "I had a tumor," she said dryly. "The doctor removed it. And yes, he gave me drugs."

"Is that why you wore the sunglasses?"

"Duh."

"Girrrllzzz!" my mother called from the back door.

"We're back here, Mom," I said, glancing at Donna's cigarette.

"Din-nerr."

"Com-minggg," we both said, in conscious imitation of my mother's exaggerated pronunciation.

The house smelled great, and everyone was standing around the table admiringly. My mother, who was not normally all that into presentation, had outdone herself. Roast goose, a vat of sauerkraut sprinkled with caraway seeds, potato dumplings, goose gravy, dinner rolls, two bottles of wine, green candles and a festive red tablecloth. Norman Rockwell does Eastern Europe.

"This looks so great, Mrs. Sullivan," said Donna while she moved into one of the available places at the table. "Thanks for including me."

A light film of anxiety broke out on my back and upper lip. I took a deep breath. I didn't want to do what I knew I was going to do. But I couldn't help it. I watched the lips of my family, smiling and talking, but I was hearing a *whoosh* of anger traveling through my nervous system.

"You're welcome, darling," said my mom, with tears of joy welling up in her eyes. Since my father's illness and my quirks, my mom had been drinking a lot of wine. We were all used to her tears for any number of reasons and didn't much react to them. This time, however, she looked so smug that you'd think she'd given birth to this meal instead of cooked it.

My dad is a teetotaling Irishman with a double chin and a reluctant smile. He was salivating over the meal before us. "Well, I'll tell you one thing . . . ," he said.

And everybody in the room finished the sentence, which he had repeated at least a million times before.

". . . anybody who goes away from this table hungry, it's their own fault!" Everybody said it but me, that is. Because I was struggling to keep calm despite the tyrants raging wildly in my head.

"Okay," said my dad. "Everybody can sit down where they're standing."

As everyone began to sit down, I went ballistic. *What's going on?* I shouted.

Everyone turned to look at me in total surprise. My skin was covered with a cold dew. The hairs on the back of my neck were standing up like straight pins. I was losing the struggle not to burst into tears.

"What *now*?" My sister looked bored.

"Now?" I screamed. "Now everybody is in the *wrong* places! How can you tell us to sit down where we're standing, Daddy? And why are you trying to do this to me?"

"Do what to you, Tara?" My father seemed to be controlling his own anger.

"Mixing me up! You don't sit there! You sit there! Like *always*."

I grabbed my father's arm between the shoulder and the elbow and lifted mightily in an attempt to physically hoist him out of his chair. "*Mom sits there like always!* And Gramma and Grampa sit there, please! Please!" I pointed to the chairs where I needed them to sit.

My poor grandparents looked so scared that they aged ten years in twenty seconds. I was like a deranged referee. I practically knocked my "tough guy" sister out of her chair. "Come on, Greta! You sit *there* like *always*

. . . and me and Donna sit here . . . just like always! What's wrong with you guys? Huh? What are you trying to do to me?" I was hollering and crying and acting as if I had just escaped from some lunatic asylum. But I couldn't let everyone sit in the wrong chairs. I *couldn't*.

"Come on, Daddy! Pleeezzze sit there. Mom! Please! Please! Just like always! Just like always. It's got to be just like always or else . . . or . . ." I was crouched on the floor crying. Everyone else was frozen in time and place.

In spite of all my other quirks, everyone was astounded by my holiday-meal outburst. My grandparents looked more scared than I did. My sister solemnly examined her reflection in the china-cabinet mirror. My mom's tears of pride had turned to fountains of pain. And even Donna, who was usually pretty casual about my rules, looked undone. It was my father who spoke first.

"Jesus, Mary and Joseph," he said. "I'm so sick of this shit." Because he'd used the Lord's name in vain, I began to pray for his soul.

"Our Father who art in Heaven—"

"That's it," my dad mumbled. He knocked a chair on its side and stormed out of the kitchen.

Within seconds he slammed his bedroom door so hard I thought the walls would crack. My mother grabbed a bottle of Jack Daniel's, my grandparents grabbed the glasses and the three of them went into the living room. Donna went home thinking I was taking more serious drugs than she was and hadn't told her. Greta and I put away the untouched food, then played

Chinese checkers and eventually ate Cheerios for Christmas dinner.

"I like Cheerios," Greta said. She smiled at me beatifically, like the Blessed Virgin. I was jealous because she was normal. "I like goose with dumplings better," she said slyly, "but I do like Cheerios."

"How come you never get mad, Greta?" I asked.

"You think I don't get mad?" she asked, as calmly and sweetly as ever.

"Yeah," I said.

"I've been suspended three times for beating people up. And two of those times were for you."

"So?"

"So, I get mad!"

"I still don't get it. You only get mad when you're *not at home*?"

"No." She thought for a long time before answering. "I get mad here. I just *act* mad outside."

I watched her calm, thoughtful face chewing her Christmas Cheerios and realized for the zillionth time that whatever it was that made me act the way I did had affected more than *my* life.

Before going to sleep that night, Greta and I sat in my bedroom and listened to our parents arguing in the front of the house. After a while I couldn't stand it and put a pillow over my head. "They're arguing about me," I said through the foam and cotton.

"Don't feel bad," she said, putting her arm around me. "You can't help it . . . right?"

"I can't! I really can't."

"I thought so."

"Why? Why did you think so?"

"Because . . . you're not crazy. And so . . . why would you *act* crazy . . . if you could help it?"

"How do you know I'm not crazy?"

Greta shrugged and looked at me with those unblinking eyes of hers.

"What *is* crazy?" I asked.

Immediately we heard something crash. Greta tilted her head toward the room in which our parents were fighting. "*That's* crazy," she said. We laughed a lot.

Greta jumped up and pulled back the curtains. "Hey, let's look at the angels!" Side by side we squinted to see into the dark backyard. "They look fierce in this light," Greta said.

She was right. They did look fierce. "They're like you," I said, thinking about all the physical fights my sister had either started or finished in her eleven years. "They're warrior angels."

"Thank you." Greta looked so proud that I suddenly realized how few compliments she got from me, or anyone. "How many of them are there?"

I quickly counted. "Three . . . seven . . . twelve . . . Fif-fif . . . uh-oh! There's fifteen!"

"So?"

"I . . . gotta go." Without stopping to put on my coat or boots, I ran into the yard and through the snow in search of a clean space. Barefoot and in my nightgown, I was freezing and crying before I even lay down and started making another angel. I waved my arms and legs like crazy. I was scared stiff, because I had no idea why I had to do this stupid, stupid thing! I just knew I had to. I'd never be able to sleep knowing that there were fifteen angels and not sixteen. It had to be an even number. It *had* to. Once again, I had no clue why.

When I ran back into the house, dripping with ice and slush, my parents and Greta were staring at me with horror. We were all afraid of what the new year would bring.

15

Kissing Doorknobs

Maybe it was the stress of the holidays, or the strain of going to the shrink again after making the sixteenth snow angel, or the guilt from shoplifting, or the irritation of Donna's newest boyfriend. I don't know what caused it. I never did. But one day in late January, as I was walking out the door to meet Donna, I stopped in front of the doorknob in our living room and . . . froze.

Before I knew what was happening, I had placed all ten of my fingers on the doorknob in a little circle with the *exact* same pressure, the way I had done before when performing my street ritual . . . *but this time I brought those fingers to my lips.*

Instantly and instinctively, I spread my lips out as wide as I could and touched all ten of my fingers to my lips with the *exact* same pressure. I don't remember what I was thinking when I did it. It was involuntary and yet voluntary. It was natural and yet unnatural. It was the birth of a ritual that would be repeated many, many times. In fact, from that day on, I was compelled to perform that ritual almost any time I came in contact with my front door. It wasn't easy. It was exacting.

If I slipped and applied more pressure with one finger than another, or if a finger fell off my lip, I'd have to do it all over again. Sometimes I'd have to stand there for a little while to get it perfect. It was hard to do.

My parents got pretty alarmed. Especially after I had been acting so normal for the past month.

"Why? Why? Why?" my mother asked over and over again, as if she was stuck on Replay.

"I don't know." And that was the truth. What I didn't say was that I had to do it. That it made me feel better to do it, even though it made me feel worse. I also didn't tell her that the big knot that used to be in my stomach was back and that the only way to untie it was to do the doorknob thing. I also didn't tell her how scared I was . . . again. I couldn't tell her that. The tyrants were back in control, and I couldn't explain why.

My mother had an anxious look on her face again. And that always made her act weird herself.

"I'm going to make you remember that that is not a pleasant thing to do, Tara," she said through gritted teeth. "You've been so much better. So much better! You *can't* start this again. I won't let you."

Employing a sort of demented Pavlovian reasoning, my mother threatened to slap me every time I did the doorknob ritual so that I would associate it with pain instead of pleasure—as if there was any pleasure involved with any of this.

"Taraaa!" she'd warn as I approached the door. But I couldn't think about her. I could only think about what I had to do. Whether I wanted to or not. I looked at the doorknob. I made a finger circle with the *exact* same pressure.

"Tara, please. Stop here." My mother's voice was pitiful.

"Don't kiss them. Please," she moaned.

I brought those fingers to my lips.

The slap hurt, but I didn't react. I just continued, even though I knew I'd have to start over. A few seconds later I heard my mother run from the room. I was free to start over, counting to myself. *One. Two. Three. Four.* In the beginning I wasn't sure where to stop, how many times was enough.

I heard my mother crying and throwing things in another room. I knew she was as scared and nervous as I was—and just as determined to follow her urges to stop me, no matter how much she didn't want to hurt me.

Seeing me act this way drove her past all her control points. She felt she had to do something. So we were on a collision course with each other. And the rest of the family became both witnesses to and victims of our destructive and debilitating war of the urges.

But even with the slapping and the hollering, the pleading and the tears, I considered myself lucky. After all, my counting and praying had subsided almost completely. And I only had to do this doorknob thing at home. If I had had to do it with every door I passed through, I would have been humiliated. Not to mention the time it would have taken.

After a few weeks, my mother's physical punishments were too much for her to endure.

"I can't stand this!" she'd beg. "Why can't you stop this?" *Slap. Slap.*

One day, after a few halfhearted slaps, she changed her ultimatum.

"I'm finished slapping you," she said in a shaky

voice. "The next time I see you doing it, I'm going to take you to the doctor—*another* doctor! Or maybe I'll just have myself committed and let you do as much of this as you want."

After her threat, I couldn't pry myself away from that darn doorknob. I did my ritual again and again and again and again and again and again for up to a half hour at a time, with tears of fear streaming down my face.

As promised, my mother took me to a new doctor.

"You've given your mother quite a scare," the new doc said to me in a kind tone of voice.

"Uh-huh," I replied, even though what I was thinking was "You think *she's* scared; try being *me*."

"Do you understand why your mother is scared?" she continued.

"Uh-huh."

"It's human nature. If we can't figure out why other people act in a certain way or do or say certain things, then we get scared of them. And it's fear that makes us do and say things we're not proud of."

Tell me about it, was what I was thinking, but I just sat there as embarrassed as heck to be there in the first place. I began to count the floor tiles.

"I think that's what happened to your mother. She slapped you because she was afraid," she said solemnly.

I was not worried about my mother slapping me. This was not about child abuse. I was worried about my mind, my thoughts. Were they my thoughts? Or had aliens planted them in my brain?

The doctor gave me a pat on the back. I tallied up seventy-five tiles while she told me that I was a good kid and that my eczema didn't look too bad.

I don't know what she told my mother privately, but afterward my mother seemed hopeful that whatever was wrong with me would just go away. She bought me ice cream, new jeans and a great sweater from The Gap and hugged me forever when she saw how cute I looked in them.

I could see that my mother was in as much pain about my problem as I was. She *needed* to believe that the doctor was right. She *needed* to believe I'd be cured. To help her out, I prayed it would go away. But I prayed silently, and that was a big improvement.

16
Chinese Food

ortune-cookie crumbs sprayed the air. My family was finished eating and eagerly splitting the cookies to set their fortunes free.

" 'Problems have solutions but love does not,' " my mother read. "What does that mean?"

My dad, who had forgotten his new glasses, held his fortune about as far from his face as possible. If he'd been able to stretch his arm to Ohio, his vision would have been 20/20. " 'You will receive important news from an unusual messenger.' "

The eagerness on their faces defined human hope. If aliens landed at the next table, they could easily have deduced that my family had been waiting their entire lives to receive the information hidden in those cookies.

" 'A little kindness is worth more than a little gold,' " read my sister. "What crap."

While they happily examined their fortunes, I continued straightening my rice and rearranging the contents of an eggroll into an acceptable pattern for consumption. That is, acceptable to me. That is, orderly, with the cabbage stretched out and the other ingredients lying neatly beside it. I didn't want to eat any mystery ingredients hidden by another unappealing wad of food. As a result, I hadn't taken one bite, and we'd been eating for almost an hour. My parents were doing their best to ignore my newest quirk.

I was getting testy, though. It took me so long to arrange and eat my meals that it had been weeks since I had eaten any dessert at all. It wasn't that I cared that much about desserts. I didn't like them as a rule. There were too many ingredients in them. And too many of those ingredients (like partially hydrogenated soybean oil and propylene glycol monoesters) didn't seem like things that should be eaten. Desserts, like Chinese food, were as a rule too complicated to dissect. More like science than sustenance. But still, I was hungry.

"Uh-oh!" Greta knocked over her Coke. "Whoops." Our plates were floating in ugly brown rivers of cola that streamed over the edges of the table and into our laps. As my parents shrugged and blotted the tablecloth and my sister grinned sheepishly, I felt a volcanic anger rising up inside of me.

Ignoring the complete disaster she'd just created, my sister grabbed the extra cookie. "Can I have yours?" she asked me.

"No," I said, just to be mean. "It's mine!"

"Okay," she said with a sly smile. She handed me the cookie, but before I could tell her for the thousandth time that I don't like people touching my food, she said, "Do you think the ink from the paper might have contaminated the cookie?"

She'd won. "Take it!" I snapped. "Go ahead. It's all yours. Eat it!"

My mother gave Greta a stern look. My sister just smiled at her and said, "Hey, you should thank me. By the time she gets to dessert I'll have gray hair and you'll be in a nursing home!"

My father must have agreed. "Come on, Tara," he said without looking at me, "eat something so that we can get out of here before the second coming of Christ, okay?" My dad was always impatient with my food arrangements after he had finished eating. The waitress returned and looked at the reformatted but uneaten food on my plate.

"Uh-oh!" she said sternly. "I hope you're not ambidextrous!"

The word hung in the air like a neon sign. Ambidextrous! She meant anorexic! My mother laughed first, but the three of us were quick to follow her lead. It was just what we all needed to break the tension that came from living with what I had.

"She is sorta ambidextrous," screamed Greta. "She doesn't eat with *either* hand!"

Walking home from the restaurant, I watched my sister's peaceful face. She was lost in her own thoughts and I realized that I'd been so self-involved that I'd never really gotten to know all that much about her.

"Mwa . . . hahaha!" My mother laughed at something my father said. A chill went through my spine. What if she died? What would life be like without her? Before I could recover from the chill I was counting frantically.

"One . . . two . . . three . . . four . . . five . . ."

My sister groaned softly. I didn't look at my parents or my sister, but I could imagine their faces. If only they understood that I was doing this for all of us.

"Tara," my sister whispered.

"Thirty-two . . . thirty-three . . ." I ignored her even though I could feel her at my right side and see her foot near mine.

"Your fortune cookie. I just opened it."

I ignored her. "Forty."

" *'Good things are coming to you soon!'* " She said it enthusiastically and without sarcasm. I managed to smile without losing count or having to start over. Of course, I doubted that good things were coming soon no matter who the cookie was meant for.

"Forty-one, forty-two, forty-three . . ." My mother had stopped laughing. They were all watching me. "Fifty, fifty-one."

Life had become hell for all of us, and I wasn't even fifteen yet.

The next doctor's gaze was invasive. It made me feel as if I was getting an X ray. I think she must have treated a lot of girls my age with eating disorders, because she wanted to talk about food all the time.

"Tell me about the rice."

"I like to line it up before I eat it. Make it neat."

"That must take a lot of time."

"Chinese food is a problem."

"Do you and your family eat out much?"

"Too much."

"Tell me about it."

"Well, for one thing, the idea of some strange person I've never seen touching my food in another room is

106

enough to make me dizzy. And I hate using public bathrooms because of the sign that says ALL EMPLOYEES MUST WASH THEIR HANDS. I mean, why is that sign necessary? Who doesn't automatically wash their hands after going to the bathroom? Especially if they're going to touch food? Especially—*especially* if they're going to touch *my* food!"

I was really worked up. The shrink, however, was as cool as if I had just recited the alphabet. I suspected that she wasn't listening. I wondered whether she had an attention deficit disorder.

"That's a good point, Tara. Go on."

"And then, I also don't eat out much because I have to rearrange my food before I eat it and that takes a lot of time." As I was talking, I was tapping my fingers against the underside of my chair. Three times to the right . . . then three times to the left . . . then again three times to the left . . . and three times to the right. I didn't know if she noticed. I did it pretty stealthily. So stealthily that it took me a while to notice what I was doing. When I did notice, I talked a lot more enthusiastically to distract her, because I'd much rather talk about messy food than my fear of tipping over from being unbalanced.

I went on. "Chinese food is pure hell. Stir-fries look like the aftermath of a hurricane. Strings of vegetables blown off their course and tangled around something that looks like—but might not be—meat."

"You're suspicious about the meat, then."

"I'm worried. About everything. But even if I wasn't, messes like that are not meals, if you ask me. And chop suey! Fried rice! It takes forever to sort those things out properly. Do you agree with me or do you think I'm nuts?"

"I don't think you're nuts."

But she didn't agree with me either.

Diagnosis: Borderline anorexia . . . anger issues.

17
Facing Facts

It was a warm spring night and my dad was watching his usual after-dinner television programs. I was trying to get out the door to meet Donna so that we could hang out at the park next to the pool and flirt with high-school boys.

Of course, in order to get out the front door I had to touch the doorknob and my lips. Usually, I had to do it thirty-three times. That was the standard number I had to perform before I could stop. Thirty-three perfect times, and at least a half hour later than I'd planned on leaving, I could finally slip out. Usually.

As I did my ritual, I tried not to look at my father. He had been trying not to look at me since that dinner over Christmas vacation, but he really couldn't ignore this. ". . . eight nine ten eleven twelve thirteen . . ."

I felt him staring at me for a long, sad time before he spoke. "Was it something your mother or I did? Something you're holding against us and taking out on yourself, Tara? If you're mad because I've spent so much time at the Legion, we can talk about it."

"Twenty-one, twenty-two . . ."

"Maybe you're still scared after my heart attack?"

Poor Daddy. I couldn't stop to talk to him. He probably already knew that.

"I love you, Tara. We all do. Please stop. Please."

". . . Twenty— where was I?" I asked. Oh, no. Oh, no. I lost count. I lost count and I spoke. Again! "One two three four five six seven eight nine ten eleven twelve thirteen . . ."

"Tara . . . please . . ." The doorbell rang. My father and I were both startled. I didn't stop my ritual, although I did try to speed it up. Eighteen. Nineteen.

"Answer the door!" my father yelled. He nervously pulled back a tiny piece of the curtain to reveal who was standing on our porch. I just kept counting evenly. Trying to ignore everything.

"It's Allan Jacobson!" he groaned. Pain and fear leaked out of my father's voice and enveloped me like a blanket. Mr. Jacobson was my father's old friend from college who was also the local high-school science teacher. A cold river of perspiration broke out on my neck. Without looking at my father's face, I could hear the horror in his voice.

"Stop it. Just stop it!" He sounded embarrassed. I continued my counting without looking at him.

"Stop it!"

"Twenty-two . . ." The bell rang again. The sweat was now running down my back.

"Answer the door!" he repeated.

I ignored him. Twenty-three.

"Answer the damn door, and I mean it. Can't you just stop it for once?"

I couldn't stop it and I couldn't answer him. I was so nervous I lost count just as he picked me up, moved me to the side and opened the door. As I looked at my

110

dad's frightened face and his friend's calm one, I was so humiliated that I burst into tears. Giant tears. Sobs, really. And as if I was a little baby my daddy took me in his arms and rocked me. Then he did something I'd never seen before. He began to cry too. His tears scared me more than my ritual. His pain was almost more than I could bear. We both cried for what seemed like hours as Mr. Jacobson sat on the couch and looked at his hands.

After my dad and I calmed down, Mr. Jacobson started asking me questions that nobody had ever asked me before.

"What does it feel like when you do that thing with the doorknob, honey?" He called me honey. I had to fight back more tears just because of that. He sounded so kind.

"I don't know," I said, and more tears poured out of my eyes. "I just know I have to do it."

"Do you do it a certain number of times?" he asked.

I was surprised. I'd never told anyone that I had to do it a certain number of times. "Thirty-three. I have to do it thirty-three times before it feels finished and I can stop. How do you know that?"

"I have a boy in my class, a little older than you, who I think has a similar problem."

I wasn't alone? I wasn't the only one in the world with this secret mental problem? I doubted it. But my father and I were both very interested. My mother and my sister, who had just walked in from shopping and missed most of the drama, could hardly believe their ears.

"What problem? What *is* the *problem*?" my mother asked somewhat hysterically.

"She kisses doorknobs," said my sister in a tone of voice that said, "She likes lemonade."

"I'm crazy," I admitted for the first time. "That's what the problem is. And Mr. Jacobson has a boy in his class who's crazy too."

"Do you enjoy the doorknob thing, Tara?" asked Mr. Jacobson.

"Of course not!" I screamed. And for the first time, I turned on my mother. "Did you hear that, Mommy! I said of course not! You thought you could make me remember that this stuff isn't pleasant by slapping me! Do I look like I'm suffering from an excess of pleasure, Mom? Do I look like a poster child for joy?"

My mother burst into tears. I immediately ran into her arms and cried softly too.

Eventually Mr. Jacobson spoke again. "I think that Tara is suffering from an obsessive-compulsive disorder."

My dad said it out loud. "Obsessive-compulsive disorder." His voice sounded flat, as though he was reading it, or not sure of the pronunciation.

"*Another* diagnosis," my mother mumbled with unconcealed hostility, and kissed my forehead. "Bullshit."

"Well, it sounds better than immaturity or self-esteem problems," my dad said softly. "Or attention deficit-immaturity-anorexia-anger. As we can all see, Tara pays attention like an adult, is a normal weight and could use a little more anger about her situation!"

"I'm sorry, Marty," my mom said. "But she's been to so many psychiatrists."

"A lot of professionals are unfamiliar with this," Mr. Jacobson said. "In fact—and I'm not an expert—from what I understand, it's not a psychological disorder; it's a chemical one."

"A chemical one?" said my parents in stereo.

"Does that mean I'm not crazy?" I asked.

My parents didn't trust themselves to venture a guess. Mr. Jacobson knelt down by my side and stroked my hair. "You're definitely not crazy, Tara," he said gently.

"How do you know?" I asked.

"Crazy would be if you enjoyed kissing the doorknobs or counting or whatever. But you definitely don't look like you're having any fun."

"That fortune cookie was right!" Greta screamed. "Remember? 'You will receive important news from an unusual messenger.' Remember? Mr. Jacobson is an unusual messenger, isn't he? And Tara's cookie said good things would come to her soon!"

12

The Open Brain Door

Mr. Jacobson must have left my house and called his student on a car phone, because ten minutes after I watched his taillights turn the corner, I was talking on the phone to a boy named Sam who told me he had what I had and promised to come over the next day after school.

I couldn't sleep all night. *He has what I have!* I couldn't pay attention to anything at school the next day. *What do I have?* I worried that he'd be crazy. *The doorknob thing?* I worried that he'd look crazy. *Counting cracks?* Then I worried that I'd look crazy. *Praying?* But when I opened my front door to meet him, all I could see was a really cute boy who didn't look crazy at all. *How could he have what I have?* He didn't even have dark circles under his eyes.

Unfortunately, I knew that I looked tired and stressed despite Kristin's makeup tips, which she had gleaned from *Today's Teen* magazine.

"Do you . . . kiss doorknobs?" I asked with too much hope in my voice by half.

"That's cute. Most people just say hello, but I'll

remember that one." As he smiled and extended his hand, my face heated up to a tropical burn. I instantly checked my arm for eczema. It was almost gone.

"I'm s-sorry!" I stammered without shaking his hand. "Hello." I backed up, tripped over nothing and banged the back of my head on the door. "Come in. I'm . . . a little . . . embarrassed here, okay?"

Sam walked in ahead of me. "Thank you. Nice doorknobs." He smiled mischievously. "You've got very good taste in hardware."

It took me a long time to laugh. I was shocked that he could make fun of something so serious.

In about a second, my mother came in and introduced herself to Sam. While they were exchanging greetings, I imagined Sam kissing doorknobs alone, then kissing them with me, maybe on opposite sides of the same door. I pictured our wedding, our honeymoon in a doorknob factory, our doorknob-kissing children and vacations spent in hardware stores.

The next thing I knew, my mother and Sam were seated on the couch and Sam was saying, "I don't kiss doorknobs. Or do anything unusual with them at all." My mother and I were both devastated. Mr. Jacobson had raised our hopes of finding a diagnosis, a cure and maybe even a community. *He has what I have!* We both shrank an inch or two from disappointment.

"But we thought . . . ," was all she managed to say. I was as mute as our doorknob.

"I was afraid of germs," Sam went on. "I used to wash my hands until they bled from all that soap and hot water. Over and over and over and over. Over and over and over again. I didn't know why. I just had to do it. And I couldn't be interrupted."

"I see," my mother mumbled to herself sadly as I brightened.

"Are you cured now?" I asked.

"Pretty much. I'm on medication now. It helps even though, for me, the medication has its own set of problems."

My mother and I were both silent.

Sam continued. "I sweat a lot now. For instance. But I don't wash it off or anything."

"It can't be the same, honey," my mom said to me. "His washing his hands is hardly as weird as your . . . things."

"Hard to say what's weirder, Mrs. Sullivan," said Sam. "We were both compelled to carry out a ridiculous action because of—"

"Tyrants," I whispered. "We've got tyrants in our heads."

"That's good." Sam was smiling. "I never thought of it that way, but that's just what it's like."

"I'm missing something," said my mother skeptically.

Sam was up to the challenge. "Obsessive-compulsive disorders have a lot of varieties. There are people with contamination fears like me. Worriers. Doubters. Counters like Tara. Those with needs for symmetry . . ."

"What's symmetry?" I asked. I'd thought I had a good vocabulary, but this guy knew some words.

"Balance. You know, if you tap with the left foot, you have to tap with the right foot to make it even."

Before my poor mother could spit out, "She doesn't have that . . . ," I bounced out of my chair and started screaming. "*Oh my God! You know what I have!*

You do have what I have! Like when you have to touch all ten fingers with the exact same pressure!"

"You've got *that too*!" shrieked my mother. None of this was good news to her. But to me it was the best thing that happened to me since eating apricot dumplings in Michigan when I was four years old. I was visible! Someone saw me! *Knew* me! Knew what I had!

Sam went on. "There's also checkers, cleaners, confessers, defilers and hoarders. They're all symptoms of an obsessive-compulsive disorder."

I lost him for a few minutes as I went through my own checklist. Symmetry. Yes. Fears. Yes. Worrying. Yes. Confessing was an easy one.

"How did we catch this?" I asked.

"We didn't catch it. We were probably born with it. And we probably inherited it from someone in our family."

"No one in my family kisses doorknobs," said my mother dully.

"Maybe they just secretly hoard things or break things or count in their heads. You probably wouldn't know. Especially if it wasn't someone who lived with you."

"I don't get it. I just don't get it," said my poor mother.

Sam pointed to his forehead. "This part of the brain, right above the eyes, is where worry is registered. Brain scans show that people with OCD have a lot of activity in this part of the brain."

"She's a worrywart. That I understand," she said gently, and put her arm through mine.

Sam continued. "Somewhere on the top of the brain is the basal ganglia. It functions as a gate for thoughts.

With most people it opens and closes after each thought is completed. A person has a thought. They do the action. The thought is gone. With people like us, the gate doesn't function right. It kinda stays open a little. And that's why we do things over and over. It's like our brain isn't quite sure that the thought or action was done or was done right or done enough. So it just keeps thinking the same thought over and over and we keep doing the same action over and over."

"The brain hiccups?" I said.

"Exactly! That's what they call it. A hiccup of the mind."

My mother and I were both stunned silent for a while.

"I'm not alone, Mom," I said in such a weird voice I wasn't sure if it was mine.

"Alone!" Sam smiled. "There's millions of us."

"Oh, my God!" My head was reeling. "Did you ever meet anyone else? I mean besides me?"

"Sure. Through my therapist I've met a lot of other formerly normal people who woke up one day and wondered whether broccoli had feelings and, therefore, experienced pain when eaten . . . and then kept wondering that same thought for years."

"Dear God," squeaked my mother.

"I've met people who live in fear that they might accidentally hurt someone else. People driven insane by the idea that maybe they already did. I've also met people who believe they're responsible for every plane, train or auto crash they hear about on the news. People who *know* they aren't responsible, but they *doubt* what they know, so they *wonder* if they are responsible."

"I'm so sorry, baby," said my mom, with tears in her

eyes. "For . . . everything." I was speechless once again.

"I also met a girl who believes that eating utensils have feelings, so she is careful never to touch them with her teeth so that she doesn't hurt them, and a boy who lines up his french fries with the biggest ones at the bottom before eating them. Every time." Sam was smiling. I was laughing. My mom looked as if she was ready to cry.

"How did you get cured?" my mother asked evenly.

"It's called exposure and response prevention therapy. It wasn't easy."

"Tara would do anything to get rid of this, wouldn't you, honey?"

My mind was racing. "Sure . . . yes. Yes."

"Even risk being exposed to what you're freaked out about . . . your doorknob for instance . . . and then have someone stop you from doing your ritual?"

"Huh?"

"Because I'm afraid of germs, I had to touch garbage . . . all kinds of it . . . three times a week with a behavior therapist."

"Yuck."

"And after I touched it, my therapist prevented me from washing my hands."

"Yuck yuck."

"Three times a week for three months until I could stand the idea of germs on my hands."

"Yuck yuck yuck," I said. And then my mother and I were silent again for a while.

Suddenly something occurred to me. "But my quirks change," I said. "I'd have to be constantly exposed and prevented from doing all kinds of stuff."

"Most people with OCD have shifting rituals," said Sam, handing a card to my mother, who looked as if she needed it herself. "My therapist."

" 'Susan Leonardi,' " she read, as if English was not her first language. "Great," she said weakly. "Thank you. Now, I think I'm going to lie down for a while."

"I've got to go," said Sam, standing up and shaking my mother's limp hand. "It was nice meeting you."

"And you too, Sam," said my mother. "Don't be a stranger."

"I won't," he said, smiling a wide, toothy smile. And then he turned his kind expression and sapphire eyes on me.

Embarrassed, I jumped up and tried to think of something to say.

Helping me, he asked, "Walk me out?"

"I'll walk you out," I said, and then just stood there as if my shoes were nailed to the carpet until he held the door open for me.

On the front porch Sam stopped and turned around and looked at me too closely for my comfort. Although he was three feet away, I suddenly felt too near him and vaguely nauseated.

"Do you remember what you were like before the tyrants moved into your head?" he asked.

"I remember."

"You can get there again," he said earnestly.

"I hope so," I said, trying to sound sure of myself.

As I turned and walked through my front door, I felt Sam watching me.

"Let me know how your therapy goes, okay?" he called.

"Thanks," I said fumbling with the doorknob. "For . . . for being so much . . . thanks."

"Hey, watch that doorknob," he joked. "I'm going to be watching you."

I blushed, resisted the doorknob with all my might, and walked inside, wondering if Sam was flirting with me and praying that I could get over my quirks.

Twenty minutes later, after pacing back and forth nervously, I went back to the doorknob. I made a perfect circle with my fingers. I touched the doorknob. I was almost certain that I was not strong enough to face my fears.

"One. Two. Three . . ."

19

Behavior Therapy

"Tell me how you'd describe your problem, Tara," Susan Leonardi began gently. I looked at both my parents for help, but they were at more of a loss than I was. I examined Susan Leonardi for a long moment before speaking.

She was a small woman with red hair and freckles. She looked like a cheerleader for crazy people. I imagined her jumping up and down in a short skirt and yelling, "Two, four, six, eight . . . you can overcome your fate!" Instead, she just calmly sipped raspberry tea on an orange floral couch and gave off earth mother vibes.

"I have . . . tyrants living in my head. They've been there since I was ten. They make me think thoughts and do things that I don't know why I do. *They* are crazy. But I have to do what they want. And I look crazy."

"I'm sorry you've been in pain for so long, Tara," Susan said gently. Then, without pity but with sympathy, she turned to my parents. "I'm sorry you've had to stand by helplessly and watch your sweet little girl be tormented by her thoughts."

A rush of emotion ran through my parents and me like an electrical impulse.

"We've been to see people," my father said softly. "Internists. Psychiatrists. Psychologists. We didn't completely bury our heads in the sand."

Susan turned back to me. "I'll bet you didn't describe it to them the way you've described it to me. Am I right, Tara?"

"I couldn't," I said. "Until my dad's friend came over and introduced me to Sam . . . I didn't feel like I had the words to describe it. It would have sounded so stupid, so unbelievable."

As my parents and I sat taking this all in, Susan smiled lightly and poured my mother some more raspberry tea. "Sam is a great kid. He worked very hard." Susan put her cup down and leaned forward. "Obsessive-compulsive disorders are neurological conditions, a biological disease, caused by a malfunction of some sort in the brain's circuitry."

My parents and I all muttered the word "disease" as if it were poison on our tongues.

"So for sure," said my mother, "it's not a psychological disorder?"

"What she means is, 'Please tell us that my daughter has an open brain door and isn't crazy!' " I said. But I said it nicely, because by then I believed that Susan Leonardi could cheer me on to the finish line, where my own thoughts were waiting for me.

"Of course, the observable aspects make it easy to see how OCD could be mistaken for a psychological disorder."

"She acts pretty crazy," said my father, and then looked ashamed of himself.

"I'm sure she does," said Susan, smiling. "Imagine how you'd act if you were trapped in an endless loop of repetitive obsessive thoughts accompanied by an anxiety so powerful you'd do anything . . . perform any compulsive act . . . just to make it go away."

We were all silent. In horror. In recognition.

"What causes it?" asked my father nervously.

"We don't know."

"That's comforting," said my dad grimly.

"Maybe genetics. Maybe chemicals in the brain. Maybe stress, trauma or other injury. Although the behavior has been around as long as man, the research is new."

My mother burst out laughing and startled all of us. "I'm sorry," she said. "I'm picturing cavemen and -women experiencing problems getting in and out of cave openings because they don't have any doorknobs to kiss." My mother's humor, her saving grace, crept back into her eyes. We all relaxed a little.

"I haven't been very . . . understanding about this," she admitted, and her eyes filled with tears.

"Obsessive-compulsive behavior is very difficult for families to cope with. In fact, nothing that we know of drives families crazier faster."

"Amen." And that was from my mother. My father put his arm around her. Susan squeezed my hand.

"Are you ready to begin the hardest work of your life?"

I nodded.

"Four years is a long time. Especially for a fourteen-year-old. The therapy is not going to be easy," she said.

"What do you mean?" I asked.

"The longer a person has been a slave to an OCD,

the harder it is to make him or herself risk freedom. I've seen people who have been suffering from OCD for twenty years. They're so used to their OCD that they don't really want to recover. Life would be too scary without it."

"Twenty years?" my mother sounded as if she was ready to cry. "People have this for twenty years?"

Despite my personal doubts, I felt an overwhelming urge to reassure my mother. "I'll do it, Mom," I said with a shaky voice. "I will."

My mother didn't look convinced. "What about medication?"

"No, please, I don't want medication," I interrupted. "You know I'm afraid to even take vitamins."

Susan Leonardi nodded. "This is a pretty common reaction from many OCD sufferers," she explained. "Why don't we move ahead with behavior therapy. If that proves inadequate on its own, then we'll consider medication. How's that?"

That night Sam called to give me his support. "So, now what do you think? Do you still think you've got the courage to face your fears?"

"I guess," I said stupidly.

"I hope so. Because if you don't, they'll just get bigger . . . and bigger . . . and bigger."

This was his idea of support? "Sam," I said quietly. "I have to hang up now."

"I scared you?"

"Yes."

"Good," he said. "Deal with it."

20

The Game Plan

I dealt with it by making a list of all the things I wanted to accomplish:

- stop the doorknob ritual
- stop praying
- stop thinking of the terrible things
  that could happen to my family
- speak on a stage
- stop counting
- stop arranging my food . . .

"This is a lot to work on," Susan said. "Are you up for it? Do you have what it takes to fight the tyrant and win?" I knew she was going to be a cheerleader.

"You're not going to make me stand up and run in place, are you?" I said lamely.

"No. You've been running in place," she said evenly.

"Good point," I mumbled.

"I want you to move on," she said gently.

"How?"

Susan took my hand. "Every day, three times a day, I want you to confront your fears by imagining your parents hurt, injured or dead."

"What!"

". . . for five minutes a day. I want you to feel the horror. Experience your pain . . . your fear and your loss . . ."

"Oh, God!"

"Then," Susan continued, "do nothing. *Don't pray, don't kiss doorknobs, don't count.* Can you do that, Tara?"

I was so nervous that I began to count the slats in her blinds.

"Are you counting?" she said.

"Are you a mind reader?" I asked.

"Sort of. Now, come on. Let's give it a try together."

"Do I have to say it out loud?"

"Are you afraid to say it out loud?"

"Yes."

"Then I'm afraid so, honey. Come on."

I shut my eyes. I was sweating already.

"I don't like behavior therapy," I said.

"Do you like kissing doorknobs? Do you like being a slave?"

"My parents are lying dead in a funeral parlor. They . . ."

"Go on . . ."

I opened my eyes, and tears fell out of them. "This can't be easy for people who don't have OCD!" I screamed.

"It isn't. But it's a lot harder for you. And if you don't do it, everything will be a lot harder for you, for the rest of your life."

"They died in a car accident. They are missing most of their heads but I know them anyway. Nothing will ever be the same again. I don't know what will happen next. I'm afraid. My mother is wearing a blue dress that she bought a few weeks ago. My father is wearing his St. Patrick's Day outfit. I don't know why. It isn't St. Patrick's Day. I hate St. Patrick. No, I don't. I'm sorry I said that; God forgive me. I just want to know why he could drive the snakes out of Ireland but not save my dad. I'm sick. I don't know how I can go on feeling this sad. I want to reverse this. I don't want this to be true. I can't have this be true."

I opened my eyes. "I don't like this game!" I screamed.

"It isn't a game, Tara. It's a fight. A fight to regain your free will."

"What's free will? Huh? What?" I started crying really hard. It was as if a dam had opened. I cried for so long that my eyes swelled shut. Saliva dripped out of my mouth. I didn't care what I looked like. I didn't want to do the behavior therapy. I just wanted to keep crying forever. Until all my bad feelings came out.

Susan waited patiently and occasionally handed me Kleenex. When I calmed down a little she spoke.

"You aren't praying, are you?"

"No!" I screamed at her.

"Are you counting?"

"I hate you!" I crumpled into a ball on the floor. I really hated this woman. I began praying.

"No!" she yelled at me. "*No* counting. No praying."

"I hate you!" I screamed again.

"That's okay," she said. "It's not important."

"I saw a report on the news about domestic violence," I hissed. "I understand now. I get it. Why battered wives go back to men who batter them!" I screamed.

"Well, then. You'd better use that and work harder," Susan said.

I hated her, but she was right. I made another vow to fight harder for my freedom so that I wouldn't find more tyrants in my life to control me. I must have made a thousand vows that day . . . and for a lot of days thereafter.

Needless to say, my first experience fighting the tyrants was daunting. And each time after that was just as hard. My parents helped by being in the room with me, but they didn't do much more than Susan. I suffered through terrible thoughts that I thought of *on purpose,* and nobody helped me! I was in hell.

I couldn't believe how hard it could be to break a habit that I hated. I went to Donna's house for comfort. Her father was hunched over his beer. He didn't even look at me. Her mother was baking and listening to old love songs. Donna couldn't stand to look at them, so we went up to her room and closed the door.

"I've got something to tell you," she said.

"What?"

"I did it with Chuck!"

"What?"

"It!"

"You mean . . ."

"Yes!"

"Why?"

"It was really sort of an accident."

"An accident?" My head was spinning. I was trying to get over the rituals that I did to protect people I loved, and now my best friend just had sex by accident.

"We kinda got carried away. We were high."

"You're fourteen years old. Fourteen years old!"

"I know how old I am, Tara!"

"You're way, way, way too young!"

"You thought I was too young to smoke too," she said smugly, and lit a cigarette. I was so mad at her I wanted to beat her up. She blew a smoke ring at me. I did not put it on my finger. I slumped on the bed next to her and put my head in her lap. Then I thought of what she'd done and moved my head down to her knees.

"Did you use a condom?"

"No. But don't worry," she said.

"Maybe you should worry," I said nervously. We sat in silence for a while and listened to her mom's radio playing what sounded like a Madonna song.

"Want me to help you with your compulsive homework?"

"No," I snapped. "I think you've got enough to worry about."

"I'm not worried. Tell me what you do. I want to help you."

I told her. All of it. She listened very carefully.

"I wanna try it," she said, and closed her eyes. "Okay, I'm picturing my parents dead." I watched her face to try to get a gauge of her pain. Her expression didn't change. She didn't speak. After about a minute she smiled and opened her eyes. "I can't. I'm getting too much pleasure out of this."

She did make me laugh. And I needed it.

Afterward, I made her come with me to the drugstore to buy condoms. "Don't embarrass me," she said as we walked into the store, "or I'm leaving."

"Better embarrassed than dead," I said seriously, and pointed to the various condom boxes.

"I don't know *how* to buy this," she whispered, and all the smug coolness had gone out of her voice.

"Can I help you girls?" asked the pharmacist.

"Um . . . no, sir," said Donna. "We're just . . ."

"Yes. We'd like to buy a box of condoms," I said.

His sixty-year-old face twitched in disapproval. Donna's fourteen-year-old face twitched in embarrassment. I was unfazed. I didn't care what it took, I was going to keep my friend from turning sex into suicide, or motherhood either. "Maybe you could recommend the best ones," I said.

"How old are you girls?" he asked very sternly. It made me mad.

"Why?" I asked. "Why do you want to know how old we are?"

"Because I want a note from your parents or I'm not selling birth-control devices to . . . ah . . . underage . . ."

"It's not for birth control," I said. "Not necessarily, that is." Donna was putting her hand in front of her face. I was unstoppable. "Okay, it is for birth control. But, more important, it's for protection. It's for lifesaving. So it's really to prevent death more than to prevent life."

"No," he said. "Not without a parent."

"But we don't have sex with our *parents*. We need the condoms to protect us when we have sex with *boys*."

With that Donna ran out of the store as if she was on fire. I followed her, but I was still addressing the pharmacist over my shoulder. "You shouldn't have done this, sir. I hope you can live with your decision." And then I went over the top and screamed, "I hope *she* can live with your decision."

I was unsuccessful in my efforts to get Donna into another drugstore after that incident. Oddly enough, I felt empowered. I had never acted so boldly . . . so even if I was still kissing doorknobs, I had fought my first bully. The behavior therapy was doing something for me.

———————

Sam called that night and I told him all about my work with Susan and nothing about Donna. It was too embarrassing. And too personal.

21
My Civil War

In school we were studying the Civil War. Our country was torn apart and brothers were killing brothers. All because some people thought they had the right to own other people.

It occurred to me that my family and my life had been torn apart because of the tyrants in my head who wanted to own me. I knew that it was a huge stretch to compare my OCD with the Civil War, but I had become a different person and my grades and friendships had suffered because invisible tyrants made me a slave to their whims. And so, as odd as this thought was, it gave me strength. Which I needed.

Because no matter how passionate I was, or how strong I decided I would be, my behavior therapy was very, very hard. I lost a lot of battles. It had been months and I was still involved in a terrible thirty-three-step dance involving my lips, fingers and a doorknob. I also still counted cracks, prayed, tapped and reconfigured my food. Not all the time. But enough of the time to doubt that I'd ever win the war for my freedom. And on the good days, when I felt as if I was making progress—I was scared then too.

I raised my hand in class for the first time in months.

"Tara," my teacher said with concealed surprise in her voice.

"I was just wondering. Do you think the slaves ever got scared after they were freed?"

"What?"

A few kids laughed.

"I mean . . . do you think that they ever said, 'Hey, never mind. Let's just go back to the way it was because . . . because I'm used to the way it was and I'm scared now?'"

"Well, that's an interesting question, Tara. I suppose so. I mean, their lives were completely uprooted and they often had nowhere to go. So I'd venture to guess that many of them longed for the security of their old ways . . . no matter how horrible . . . in exchange for the frightening freedom they were being faced with."

"But they did it," said Keesha, as if she'd read my mind. "They coped." The classroom exploded with laughter. I never could slip anything past Keesha. I loved that about her. I was embarrassed but vowed to myself to work harder.

When the bell rang and my class hit our lockers I grabbed her arm. "Keesha?"

Keesha froze dramatically.

"Wanna walk home together?"

Keesha was speechless. It was kind of funny. Because she always had a wisecrack answer for everything, her nonresponse made me know that she was willing to be my friend again. I was so happy that I hugged her. And when Anna saw me hugging Keesha she approached us.

"What's going on?" she asked carefully.

"I—I think I can walk with you guys again. I think. I'm not sure. B-But I want to try," I stammered. "Will you let me try?"

Keesha and Anna both smiled so big that I could practically see myself in their braces.

I stepped on every crack I could find. I felt nervous, dizzy, sick, but I did it while Anna and Keesha cheered for me.

"*Damn!*" Keesha said, testing me.

"In the name of the Father and the Son and the Holy Ghost . . ." I prayed. They frowned. When I was finished I shrugged and jumped on a crack. "*So!*" I shrieked happily. "Maybe I'm doin' cracks first!"

My friends jumped on cracks too. When we passed the hardware store I got an idea and ran inside. "Come on," I yelled.

Standing in front of a wall of doorknobs, I looked at my distorted reflection, then at Keesha's and Anna's. They didn't know about my doorknob ritual. It had been as carefully guarded as any of my secrets. Now I didn't care if they knew. I felt giddy. As a test, I ran my hand across a few of the doorknobs. Even though I only had to do the ritual on my front-door doorknob, I would have never tried a stunt like this before. Especially in front of my friends, just in case it triggered a new ritual. But here I was. I felt nothing, and jumped for joy.

"Something tells me this is one ritual I don't want to know about," said Anna.

"I second that," said Keesha, looking at her teeth in doorknob extreme close-up.

We ran back outside and skipped down the street arm in arm.

"Hey," said Keesha. "What about the dolls? The ugly short fat naked dolls?"

"My trolls!" I laughed. "They've been put away for months. Get with the program!"

By the time we got to the block where Anna turned off, we were all holding hands and jumping for joy. We were friends. We had history together. We'd survived a test.

"Thank you, you guys. Thank you for being here for me." I thought of Kristin and stopped jumping.

"How's Kristin?"

"In New York," said Anna. "She's a Glamour Do. The cover, too, I think."

We jumped for her. Then Keesha stopped jumping and turned to Anna.

"Is Kristin eating?" asked Keesha.

"I don't think so. Her manager told her he likes it that she's thin," said Anna.

Keesha looked grave. "In that case, she really ought to eat her manager."

I felt scared for Kristin. Actually, the fear barely had time to register before I was counting cracks again.

"Damn!" said Keesha.

For the rest of the way home, I did my best to pray for Keesha and count cracks at the same time. It was hard.

22
Sam

Sometime around my sixth week of behavior therapy, Sam rang my doorbell instead of my phone. Before I could speak he said, "So . . . do you still . . . kiss doorknobs?"

"Ah, most people just say hello," I gushed, playing along, "but I'll remember that one."

"I'm s-sorry!" he stammered. "Hello." He backed up, tripped over nothing and banged the back of his head on nothing in perfect imitation of me at our first meeting.

I doubled over with laughter. "Come in. I'm . . . a little . . . embarrassed, okay?"

"Thank you. Nice doorknobs." He smiled mischievously, walking by me. "You've got . . ." and then I joined him and we both said, "very good taste in hardware."

He was taller than I remembered but every bit as cute. "You look good, Tara," he said, once again standing a little too close for my comfort. I backed up. I could feel my face flushing, but Sam either didn't notice or ignored my embarrassment. "Let's see, I don't see any lip gloss on your doorknob, so . . . your therapy must be going well."

"Ha!" was all I could manage. An expulsion of air. More like a cough than a laugh.

"I brought you something," he said, pulling a box from his pocket and handing it to me.

"You did?" I asked stupidly. "Why?"

"You'll see. If you open it, that is."

Nervously I took the lid off the box, pulled back the purple tissue paper and burst out laughing. It was a crystal doorknob! And all around it were chocolate kisses wrapped in silver paper.

"Do you like it?" Sam asked with mock seriousness. "I know you're very particular about your hardware, so I was a little nervous selecting one."

"I . . . I love it. It's the funniest present I ever got."

"It's a celebration. Of your challenge. Of your strength. And of your options." Sam snatched a candy kiss from the box. "If you don't mind."

Stunned, I watched him unwrap the kiss and offer it to me.

"Take a bite," he said. "But just a bite. Not all of it."

"Why?"

"Contamination therapy. Refresher course."

"Okay." I took a tiny bite and Sam popped the rest of it into his mouth.

"Just to keep me on my toes."

Before I could respond to his joy, he took the doorknob out of the box and offered it to me. "You don't need to kiss this, do you?" he asked, and I shook my head, trying not to smile. Then he held it up to the light and turned it. It picked up color from everywhere.

It changed before my eyes. And it kept changing. I couldn't miss the symbolism.

"This is so nice of you!" I was in shock.

"You're welcome," he said.

"Thank you," I said.

"You're welcome," he said again, and he handed me the doorknob and flopped into a chair. "So . . . how've you been?" he asked with a big smile.

"I . . . I'm . . . good. I'm good," I stammered.

"You're good?" He smiled. "That's good that you're good. Because today is the one-year anniversary of the first time I could stand being hugged," he said simply. "So I wanted to celebrate with someone who knows what it means."

He stood up and held out his arms. I was so embarrassed I thought I'd die. Donna was having unsafe sex and I couldn't even hug a boy celebrating his victory over contamination fears without going completely spastic.

I took the long step into his arms, gave him a little hug and then tripped over nothing backing out of it again. He smiled sweetly and then sat on my couch.

"So . . . how's life with Susan Leonardi?"

"I hate it and I hate her."

"Good. Let's get some ice-cream sodas and toast to hating Susan Leonardi . . . the woman who reintroduced us to free will."

On the way to the ice-cream parlor Sam told me funny stories about his group therapy. We laughed again about the girl who thought eating utensils had feelings.

"Still?" I asked.

"Well, she says she still thinks that they have feelings

but now she thinks they're less sensitive than she origi-
nally thought."

"Huh?"

"So sometimes she bites her spoons and forks just for
fun. To play with them." Sam punctuated his story by
taking my hand and biting my finger. I felt squishy
with pleasure.

"Sam!" We turned around and saw the pharmacist
standing in front of his shop. He was looking at me as
though I was a stripper or a prostitute or something.

"Hi, Uncle Joe," said Sam casually. I thought I'd die.
Uncle Joe.

"Oh, sorry. Uncle Joe, this is my friend Tara. Tara,
this is my Uncle Joe."

"We met," he said, and his eyes were steel.

"Oh, sure," said Sam. "You know everyone."

"No. I don't think I know your parents, do I, Tara?"
he asked.

"No, sir," I said. Uncle Joe and I held each other's
eyes defiantly in a silent war for what we both believed
was right. Uncle Joe looked away first. I was dizzy with
my own joy.

"Nice seeing you, Sam. Say hello to your parents."
Uncle Joe went back into his store. Sam looked confused.

"It's a long story," I said. And one I didn't want to
tell, since it was really about Donna's private life.

Over ice-cream sodas I told Sam all about my therapy and realized that he was the first person who *knew*
how hard it was, who understood exactly what I was
going through.

On the way home we stopped in the park, lay down
in the grass and looked up at the sky.

"What are you thinking?" I asked him.

"I'm not telling you," he said in a teasing voice.

"Why not?"

"Because you won't believe me anyway."

He was right. I probably wouldn't have. But all of a sudden it didn't matter so much that I would never be able to know his thoughts.

"What are *you* thinking?" he asked me.

"I'm not telling you."

"That's all right," he said, and turned on his side to look at me. I could smell the slightly sweet smell of ice cream on his breath.

"It is?" I teased.

"Yeah. Because I can live with that uncertainty."

And then he kissed me. An intense, warm, firm connection that traveled through my system on every nerve ending I had.

"Was that part of your contamination therapy?" I asked, forcing a lightness into my voice that I didn't feel.

"I guess it is. Thanks. You've helped me a lot."

"Are you going to have to do this again and again and again?" I asked with an almost straight face.

"I think so," he said with an even straighter face.

23
Living with It

I think I figured out my dream.

It's a warm, sunny summer day. My friends and I are happily playing outside my house. We're chasing each other and laughing. We all feel safe and happy. Then, out of nowhere, a giant monster pops up from behind a white house a block away. It is huge and fearsome and blocks out most of the blue sky. It is so big that in one step it will not only be at my house, it will be on my house, possibly crushing us to death. We all scream and run. I can't run.

As I look at it now, it's kind of obvious. That monster was my OCD. It came out of nowhere, blocked out my world and threatened to crush me. As much as I cried, I couldn't run. I was paralyzed.

As it turns out, living with doubt is a lot less painful than trying desperately to live without it. Somebody said that a coward dies a thousand deaths but a brave man dies just once.

Because of my OCD, I had been trying so hard not to be afraid, I was hardly living at all. When I finally faced my fears and doubts, unbelievably, they became boring and then they went away.

Sometimes I'm mad that I had to have OCD, but

then I remember that I didn't get to pick it. It's like my blond hair, green eyes and eczema—it picked me.

And I am happy that I was finally able to choose not to let it control me. I'm very proud of that.

My old friend Kristin is on the covers of *Glamour*, *Seventeen* and *Teen*. I'm proud of that too, despite the sacrifices she's making that I don't agree with.

Anna, Keesha and I have resumed our relationship and walk to and from high school together every day. I love high school and I'm very, very proud that I can walk to and from it with my friends.

My relationship with my parents is a lot better. Actually, now that they don't have to fight over me anymore, *their* relationship is a little worse. As it turned out, focusing on their own problems was not much easier for them than focusing on mine. But I don't worry about it as much as I used to. And I try to stay out of my mother's thoughts, no matter what they are.

My sister has been freed from having to beat people up for me, since I don't act quite as nuts anymore. She seems a little bored now, though. I think she misses her old role as my heroine. Keesha says Greta should put her talent to use teaching a self-defense class to people who have been mugged. Anna thinks Paulo should come back to town just to take Greta's class. We still laugh about Paulo a lot.

Donna got pregnant and went to live in a special school for "expectant" high-school girls on the other side of the city. I take the train to visit her there every Saturday. I miss her a lot, but I especially miss her on the train because I remember how much fun we used to have taking it downtown together. Donna misses me too and is always excited when I walk into that ugly green "family room" where she spends most of her time.

The school is an old convent, and even though nuns don't live there anymore, the building looks as if it has taken a vow of poverty if not chastity. The hallways are drafty, the banisters are loose and the paint is chipping. I always feel like holding my breath there, and I think that's a normal response.

"Tara!" Donna screamed as she waddled toward me the first Saturday I visited. "Oh, my God, you look so *pretty*!"

"Nah." I smiled shyly and touched Donna's belly, which was the size of a Volkswagen. "I just look thin to you."

"Well?" she asked, hands on hips and pretending dismay. "Did you bring me candy?"

"Gummy worms . . . just like you asked for." Donna's face lit up with joy. Simultaneously she dove into the bag of colorful gelatinous worms and pulled me down on a plastic couch. She was smiling from ear to ear. Colorful gummy worms hung out of the sides of her mouth. I'd never seen her look so young or so happy. I sat down next to her and examined her face.

"So . . . you look good," I said.

"I'm fat!"

"Not really," I said.

"You know, maybe it's the hormones, but I'm very happy. And I kinda like this place."

I looked around at the plastic furniture, dusty miniblinds and Sony Trinitron television tuned to a talk show and wondered what it was she liked.

"I know it doesn't look like much," she said in response to my expression, "but the people are real nice here."

"That's good," I said lamely. Donna stopped inhaling gummy worms and lit a cigarette. I grabbed it out of her mouth and put it out. "How selfish can you be?" I asked her. "Unless you've swallowed an oxygen tank for that baby, you better not be trying to poison it."

"I think those tyrants are still inside you," she said, smiling.

"Maybe. But they're weaker. For instance, I don't blame myself for *your* pregnancy anymore."

"Who do you blame?" she teased. We both yelled, *"Uncle Joe!"* and laughed.

"So have you decided what to do?" I asked.

"No," she said. "I don't know what's the matter with me, but every time I think I can give it up I feel sick, and every time I think about taking it home with me, to live in my parents' house and maybe become a little me—I feel sick. I'm so glad I've got you," she said tearfully.

"Me too," I said.

"How's your OCD?"

"Okayokayokayokayokay."

We both laughed. I hugged her, kissed her cheek and told her I loved her. I thought about meeting her in the rain on that July day a year and a half earlier. I thought about the wishes she made when we sat on her roof. I hoped she'd get some of her wishes. We both knew her life was about to get very hard no matter what she chose to do with the baby.

As for my own life, I'm still battling my civil war against the tyrants. The good news is that, at least for now, I've stopped the doorknob ritual, the praying, the terrible thoughts, the counting and the lining up of my food. I haven't spoken on a stage yet, but that's the least of my worries. I do behavior therapy whenever I feel the thoughts and urges returning and occasionally see Susan Leonardi for support.

Life seems so odd to me now. The people who love us can't always help us. And the people who do help us sometimes need more in return than we're capable of giving. I'm speaking of Sam.

Apparently, his parakeet died a few days after we kissed. Suddenly he became very worried about the germs responsible for the bird's death. He didn't call me and didn't take my calls. I had no idea that his fears were escalating in a terrible cycle. When Susan finally told me what was happening to him I went to his house and rang the bell . . . again and again.

Finally Sam opened the inside door about six inches. He was wearing a mask and gloves. He looked at me with the saddest gaze I'd ever seen and didn't say a word. Trying to remain calm, I stammered, "So . . . you . . . kiss parakeets, huh?" In silence, Sam lowered his eyes. I blundered on. "I know most people just say hello, but . . ."

"I'm s-sorry!" he stammered so quietly that I could barely hear him.

The screen door separated us. I tried to open it. It was locked. "Nice doorknobs," I said evenly. "You've got good taste in—"

"Stop it!" he cried, and I let go of the doorknob.

"Then open the door, Sam. Let me in."

"I . . . can't," he whispered.

We both stood silently for a moment, considering

our mutual dilemma. "I didn't know OCD could come back this . . . bad," I said quietly.

"Apparently, *it* can do whatever *it* wants." He sounded and looked defeated.

"You can beat this," I said calmly.

"Think so?" he said earnestly.

"I know so."

"Tell me again," he said, surprising me.

"You're asking *me* for assurances? Me?"

He laughed at the irony. So did I. Then we shrugged.

"You look skinny," I said.

"I'm having a very hard time eating . . ."

"You don't think eating utensils have feelings, do you?" I asked.

"No. But I think they may have poisons on them. Or the plates may be dirty. Or the food could be contaminated or unsterilized. I . . . don't believe it, of course, but . . . I can't seem to make myself take that risk."

My heart sank. "It sounds awful. How're your parents handling it?"

"My mother's decided to take antianxiety medication because my anxiety has given her so much anxiety."

I laughed. He didn't. He backed away from the screen, afraid of my breath, my germs.

After a moment, I put my hand up to the screen. Sam vaulted back about two feet. I could barely see him.

"Do you remember what you were like before you got afraid of germs?" I asked.

"Leave me alone, Tara."

147

"Or where you were when you hugged me? Kissed me?"

"I'm trying. I'm going back to therapy," he whispered. "I hope this is a temporary relapse, but . . . it's . . . very . . . strong."

I put my other hand on the screen. "So are you. You've already proved that."

"This is worse."

"Oh. So you don't have the courage to face your fears, after all . . . if it's harder this time?"

"Don't push me, Tara. You know how scary this is."

I put both hands on the screen and recited what he had once told me. "You *have* to risk being afraid. You know that. And you have to do it because if you don't, the fears will get bigger and bigger."

The door slammed in my face. I was stunned, then furious as Sam hollered at me from the other side of the big wooden door. *"Go away, Tara . . . leave me alone!"*

Suddenly I thought of the carnival and felt my mother's frustrated rage flow through my body. I wished I could fight Sam's tyrants for him, but I knew I couldn't.

"Fine!" I screamed through the door. "Stay there! Paralyzed. Miss your own life because you're a coward."

Within a second, the door slowly opened a few inches. Sam stood in the shadow; only his mask and gloves were visible. I put my hands back on the screen. Both of them. Palms open. "I'm sorry, Sam. I just want to help you. Like you helped me."

"Don't be so superior . . . this could happen to you." His voice was cracking with pain.

"I know," I said softly. "And if it does, I'm gonna

need every bit of strength I've got. And the help of everybody I've got. That means you too. So come on."

Sam's hands met mine. Screen and gloves between us where we were touching. He was crying. I was crying. It was hard. But with this small gesture, we were fighting back. We weren't paralyzed . . . or crushed by the monster. We didn't fold or drop out. We summoned the courage to play the cards life had dealt each of us. Reluctant, insecure warriors but warriors all the same. And we weren't alone.

ABOUT THE AUTHOR

Terry Spencer Hesser is an award-winning feature writer, playwright, and independent television producer. Among her honors are the CBP Gold Award for television excellence and three Emmy nominations.

Although *Kissing Doorknobs* is not an autobiography, Hesser drew on her own experience as an adolescent in writing her story. She hopes that sharing her terror and the bafflement and despair of her parents will help others who wrestle with the "tyrants in their heads." While researching this condition, she served on the Obsessive Compulsive Foundation of Metropolitan Chicago.

Terry Spencer Hesser lives in Chicago with her husband and daughter.

AFTERWORD

by A. J. Allen, M.D., Ph.D.
Director, Pediatric OCD & Tic Disorders Clinic
Institute for Juvenile Research
Department of Psychiatry
University of Illinois at Chicago

In *Kissing Doorknobs,* Terry Spencer Hesser has provided a sensitive, moving and frighteningly accurate account of one young woman's struggles with OCD. Beginning with Tara's seemingly innocent first symptoms, we follow her and her family in their sad saga as Tara battles the disabling "tyrants in her head" while her parents haul her from one doctor to another, receiving multiple incorrect diagnoses and ineffective treatments. The family is terrified that Tara might be "crazy" and that the parents may be to blame. It is years before Tara is accurately diagnosed and receives appropriate treatment. Unfortunately, this tale is still all too familiar to those with OCD and their families and friends. But the situation is improving.

If you are reading this book because you have OCD, or because you have a friend or relative with OCD, you may have many questions about this condition. The following paragraphs try to answer some of your questions and point the way to more information and support.

OCD is short for obsessive-compulsive disorder. Obsessions are recurrent, intrusive, disruptive thoughts that cause severe distress and anxiety for individuals afflicted with them. According to many surveys, the most common obsession is a fear of dirt, germs, chemicals, or other contaminating substances. Other frequent obsessions include doubting one's memory or one's senses, fear of harm coming to oneself or others, a need to do things "just so" or "just right," concerns with symmetry, and moral or religious fears. Compulsions are repetitive behaviors or rituals, either physical or mental, that are usually intended to minimize the anxiety caused by the obsessions. Given the prevalence of contamination fears, it is not surprising that decontamination rituals, such as hand-washing and cleaning, are the most common. Other common compulsions include checking, counting, avoiding anxiety-provoking triggers, seeking reassurance (from family, friends, teachers and others), ordering and straightening, doing penance and praying. Like Tara and Sam, many children and adolescents with OCD have several different obsessions and compulsions at the same time. For example, Tara combines a counting ritual with avoidance of cracks in the sidewalk. Another feature of OCD Tara demonstrates is that the thoughts and rituals change over time, with the intensity of symptoms fluctuating and new symptoms replacing old ones.

Except for some children, a key feature of OCD is that the person with OCD possesses insight—he or she realizes that the obsessions and compulsions are excessive and unreasonable and that most people do not share these fears and rituals. Another essential feature of OCD is that the obsessions and compulsions must either significantly interfere with a person's life or cause emotional distress. The end result, as Tara and Sam clearly demonstrate, is that people with OCD want to help themselves, to resist the thoughts and behaviors, but they do not because of the pure, unremitting, unforgiving fear that is OCD. In severe cases, even as simple a task as opening a door to greet a friend may become impossible.

At one time, OCD was thought to be very rare. But a number of studies have demonstrated that it is relatively common, affecting about 1 out of 100 children and adolescents. The condition is even more common in adults, with about 1 out of 40 suffering from OCD. Many children and adolescents with OCD also have other psychiatric conditions, such as attention-deficit hyperactivity disorder (ADHD), motor or vocal tic disorders (including Tourette's syndrome), depression, other anxiety disorders, various learning disabilities (dyslexia, etc.) and oppositional behaviors. OCD increases the risk for alcohol and drug abuse and dependence, though many believe that effective treatment of the OCD lessens this risk. Many of the above conditions are discussed in *It's Nobody's Fault* (see Resources).

Sam's discussion of the causes of OCD, including the role of the basal ganglia and genetics, is accurate (though the basal ganglia actually lies deep within the brain, not on top of it). Because OCD is caused by a problem with the brain, it is often described as a neurobiological illness. The OC Foundation in Milford, Connecticut, can provide interested readers with more information in this area.

The preferred treatment for OCD is behavior therapy, when

available, in the form of exposure and response prevention (ERP). This is the therapy Tara and Sam have. The person with OCD challenges the OCD directly, exposing himself or herself to triggers of the obsessions and then preventing the compulsions. The person learns that in the course of an hour or so the OCD will "tire out" and the anxiety will fade away. While ERP eventually gives the OCD sufferer power over the disorder, the process can be very frightening. One important variation on ERP has the child or adolescent make a list of obsessions and compulsions from less severe to more severe. Then the child or adolescent does ERP, working up the list from the less severe symptoms to the more severe ones. This is often easier and less intimidating for the person with OCD, and it encourages the person by promoting early successes in therapy. Another variation is to use cognitive therapy with the behavior therapy. In this version, the OCD sufferer is taught to recognize that the obsessions are the distorted thoughts and fears behind the rituals; then the sufferer uses this knowledge to counter the fears at the same time he or she does ERP. Behavior therapy may be done once a week or on a more intensive basis. When it is done weekly, some relief is often seen in a month or two. Professional and self-help manuals for behavior therapy are available from the OC Foundation.

Medications are another option for the treatment of OCD. They are generally recommended when behavior therapy is not available, or if a person cannot do behavior therapy for some reason, or in more severe cases. The medications most often used in children and adolescents are clomipramine (Anafranil), fluoxetine (Prozac), fluvoxamine (Luvox), paroxetine (Paxil), and sertraline (Zoloft). Medications can be very helpful in suppressing the symptoms of OCD, but they don't "cure" OCD, and many people still have significant obsessions and compulsions. In addition, medications often take several weeks or months to work. The OC Foundation recently developed an excellent pamphlet on medications for OCD in children and adolescents.

The treatment of OCD doesn't end with behavior therapy or medications. OCD hurts more than just the child or adolescent who suffers from it—as is obvious from Tara's story. Parents and siblings are drawn into rituals or forced to endure them. Resentment, fear and shame are all common. The effects of OCD on the family are so profound that some people call it a family disease, and family therapy is often required. A new and excellent book on this subject is *Obsessive Compulsive Disorder: New Help for the Family* (also in Resources).

Two other aspects of a child's or adolescent's life that are frequently disrupted by OCD are peer relationships and school. Problems in both areas must be dealt with to help the OCD sufferer recover. Peer support groups may be helpful, along with education of selected friends or classmates. Regrettably, materials in this area are only now being developed. Most are available from the OC Foundation. The OC Foundation also has some excellent materials for teachers and other school personnel. (Some are listed in Resources.)

The best news for those who suffer from OCD and their families and friends is that our knowledge of OCD is rapidly expanding. For example, there is some evidence that some types of infections may trigger OCD in children and adolescents via the body's immune system. New information of this type may lead to new tests and new treatments for OCD.

There is help and there is hope for those who suffer from "the doubting disease." The following resources should help you to find it. Good luck to you and your loved ones!

Resources

The following organizations are sources of information on OCD and related conditions.

OC Foundation, Inc.
P.O. Box 70
Milford, CT 06460-0070
(203) 878-5669
Fax: (203) 874-2826
http://pages.prodigy.com/alwillen/ocf.html
The major organization for those with OCD and their families. Be sure to ask about local affiliates in Chicago, Philadelphia, Rhode Island, St. Paul (Minnesota), Texas, Michigan, and Boston. Extensive list of publications, tapes and videos, including all the major works for laypeople. Many other activities to help those with OCD and their families, including an annual conference and periodic newsletter. Anyone who has OCD, who has a family member or friend with OCD or who works extensively with individuals with OCD should belong.

Anxiety Disorders Association of America
6000 Executive Blvd., #513
Rockville, MD 20852
301-231-9350
http://www.adaa.org

Tourette's Syndrome Association, Inc.
42-40 Bell Boulevard
Bayside, NY 11361-2820
800-237-0717
http://neuro-www2.mgh.harvard.edu/tsa/tsamain.nclk
The main organization in the area of Tourette's syndrome, a condition often found with OCD in children and adolescents. Extensive publication list, newsletters, conferences; some material on OCD. Local affiliates across the country.

Children & Adults with Attention Deficit Disorder
(CH.A.D.D.)
499 Northwest 70th Ave., Suite 109
Plantation, FL 33317
305-587-3700
http://www.chadd.org/
The main organization in the area of attention-deficit disorder and hyperactivity, both of which often coexist with OCD. Some publications, local groups.

The following organizations are larger and include many conditions besides OCD.

National Alliance for the Mentally Ill (NAMI)
200 North Glebe Rd., Suite 1015
Arlington, VA 22203-3754
800-950-NAMI
http://www.nami.org/
The largest and most powerful mental health advocacy group in the United States. Affiliates across the country. Politically active locally and nationally in addressing the needs of those with any serious mental illness, including OCD.

Federation of Families for Children's Mental Health
1021 Prince Street
Alexandria, VA 22314-2971
703-684-7710
http://www.ffcmh.org/
Parent-run organization that publishes a newsletter and holds conferences. Advocates nationally in areas such as educational policy.

Many publications on OCD are available from the OC Foundation (above). A few that I often recommend are listed below:

The Boy Who Couldn't Stop Washing, Judith L. Rapoport, M.D., Signet/Penguin Books, 1989. One of the first books on OCD for laypeople. Has become a classic in the OCD community.

When Once Is Not Enough, Gail Steketee, Ph.D., and Kerrin White, M.D., New Harbinger Publications, 1990. An excellent self-help book, though slightly dated. Includes good discussion of older medications.

Getting Control: Overcoming Your Obsessions and Compulsions, Lee Baer, Ph.D., Plume/Penguin Books, 1991. Another excellent self-help book.

It's Nobody's Fault, Harold S. Koplewicz, M.D., Time Books, 1996. A layperson's guide to psychiatric conditions affecting children and adolescents. Includes chapters on OCD, Tourette's syndrome, and related disorders. Also discusses treatments.

Learning to Live with OCD—for Family Members, Barbara L. Van Noppen, M.S.W., OC Foundation. A must-have guide for families.

School Personnel: A Critical Link in the Identification, Treatment, and Management of OCD in Children and Adolescents, Gail B. Adams, Ed.D., and Marcia Torchia, R.N., OC Foundation. A must-have guide for schools.

Teaching the Tiger, Marilyn P. Dornbush, Ph.D., and Sheryl K. Pruitt, M.Ed., Hope Press, 1995. Valuable guide for schools dealing with students with OCD, Tourette's syndrome, or attention-deficit hyperactivity disorder.

Obsessive Compulsive Disorder: New Help for the Family, Herb Gravitz, Ph.D., Healing Visions Press, 1998; (800) 718-7080. A very well-done book for families "under the influence of OCD." Includes a plan to address family needs.